KONOSUBA: GOD'S BLESSING ON THIS WONDERFUL WORLD!

You Good-for-Nothing Quartet

4

NATSUME AKATSUKI

ILLUSTRATION BY
KURONE MISHIMA

YEN ON
NEW YORK

KONOSUBA: GOD'S BLESSING ON THIS WONDERFUL WORLD! 4

NATSUME AKATSUKI

Translation by Kevin Steinbach
Cover art by Kurone Mishima

This book is a work of fiction. Names, characters, places, and incidents are the product of the author's imagination or are used fictitiously. Any resemblance to actual events, locales, or persons, living or dead, is coincidental.

KONO SUBARASHII SEKAI NI SHUKUFUKU WO!, Volume 4: NAMAKURA QUARTETTO
Copyright © 2014 Natsume Akatsuki, Kurone Mishima
First published in Japan in 2014 by KADOKAWA CORPORATION, Tokyo.
English translation rights arranged with KADOKAWA CORPORATION, Tokyo, through TUTTLE-MORI AGENCY, INC., Tokyo.

English translation © 2017 by Yen Press, LLC

Yen On
1290 Avenue of the Americas
New York, NY 10104

Visit us at yenpress.com
facebook.com/yenpress
twitter.com/yenpress
yenpress.tumblr.com
instagram.com/yenpress

First Yen On Edition: December 2017

Yen On is an imprint of Yen Press, LLC.
The Yen On name and logo are trademarks of Yen Press, LLC.

The publisher is not responsible for websites (or their content) that are not owned by the publisher.

Library of Congress Cataloging-in-Publication Data
Names: Akatsuki, Natsume, author. | Mishima, Kurone, 1991– illustrator. | Steinbach, Kevin, translator.
Title: Konosuba, God's blessing on this wonderful world! / Natsume Akatsuki ; illustration by Kurone Mishima ; translation by Kevin Steinbach.
Other titles: Kono subarashi sekai ni shukufuku wo. English
Description: First Yen On edition. | New York, NY : Yen On, 2017– Contents: v. 1. Oh! my useless goddess!—v. 2. Love, witches & other delusions!—v. 3. You're being summoned, darkness—v. 4. You good-for-nothing quartet
Identifiers: LCCN 2016052009 | ISBN 9780316553377 (v. 1 : paperback) | ISBN 9780316468701 (v. 2 : paperback) | ISBN 9780316468732 (v. 3 : paperback) | ISBN 9780316468763 (v. 4 : paperback)
Subjects: | CYAC: Fantasy. | Future life—Fiction. | Adventure and adventurers—Fiction. | BISAC: FICTION / Fantasy / General.
Classification: LCC PZ7.1.A38 Ko 2017 | DDC [Fic]—dc23
LC record available at https://lccn.loc.gov/2016052009

ISBNs: 978-0-316-46876-3 (paperback)
978-0-316-46877-0 (ebook)

10 9 8 7 6

LSC-C

Printed in the United States of America

KONOSUBA: GOD'S BLESSING ON THIS WONDERFUL WORLD!

You Good-for-Nothing Quartet

Hey there! The color pages of this volume reflect the original Japanese orientation, so flip to the end of the book and read backward!

Characters

Darkness
Age 18
Job — Crusader

A female knight who specializes in defense and enjoys being beaten up by monsters. Daughter of the Dustiness family, a powerful noble house. Special skill: fantasizing.

Aqua
Age Unknown
Job — Arch-priest

A goddess who gives guidance to the young and deceased. Goes to a parallel world with Kazuma to defeat the Demon King. Likes wine. Special skill: party tricks.

Megumi
Age 14
Job — Arch-wizard

Exceptionally talented, even by Crimson Magic Clan standards. Obsessed with the überpowerful spell Explosion, she is neither capable of nor interested in using any other magic. Favorite thing: Explosion. Special skill: Explosion. Hobby: Explosion.

Yunyun
Age 13
Job — Arch-wizard

Wiz
Age 20
Job — Shopkeeper

Kazuma Satou
Age 16
Job — Adventure

An adventurer and *hikikom* (in any world) who broug Aqua to their current pla Has already given up defeating the Demon King.

Eris
Age Unknown
Job — Goddess

Sena
Age 20
Job — Government Prosecutor

KONOSUBA: GOD'S BLESSING ON THIS WONDERFUL WORLD! 4

You Good-for-Nothing Quartet

CONTENTS

The gentle glow of the hearth fire warmed my soul just to look at it.

I was watching it from the couch, lounging in a fur robe.

With an elegant motion, a hand offered me a teacup as I gazed at the fire.

"I made a cup of the finest black tea, Kazuma, my friend," Aqua said as I took it from her and she sat down beside me.

I took a sip…

"…This is just hot water."

"Oh my. What a silly thing I've done. I'm sorry, dear Kazuma."

"No worries. You can just try again. Thank you, Aqua. I'm happy with this."

I recalled that Aqua naturally purified any liquid she touched, whether she meant to or not. She must have accidentally turned the tea into plain water while she was preparing it.

But I was too relaxed to be upset about it.

The boiled water warmed my body from the inside out.

Ahhh. Peace and quiet.

What a pleasant life a person could live when they had plenty of money.

I smiled over at Aqua, who was reading a book entitled *Even a Goblin Can Learn Celebrity Lingo!*

I put the second cup of tea from Aqua to my lips.

…Hot water again. Oh well. Far be it from me to let such a minor thing get under my skin.

> ## May We Bid Farewell to This Troublesome Physical World!

1

Spring.

The season when the snow melts and all the adventurers who have shut themselves indoors come out again.

Monsters roam free once more. It's a season of flourishing.

And—

"No way! Uh-uh! It's still cold outside! What's wrong with you? Are you both stupid? There's still snow on the ground—why are you in such a hurry to go outside? Are you children? Are you little kids who wanna go play in the snow? If you're that eager, then you two go have at it!"

—it's the season when the warmth makes everyone a little, well, balmy.

Yes, it was spring, but there was still snow around town.

Aqua clung desperately to the couch as Darkness and Megumin struggled to peel her off it.

As monsters were emerging from hibernation, they felt it was time to go on a quest. Aqua had vehement objections, based largely on the temperature.

"Who is being a child here? I believe it is you, Aqua! Come on, we're going! You spent all winter lazing about. It's time to start moving again. Or else—"

"Frogs and all kinds of other monsters are starting to show up outside town. Word is, they're damaging the farms. It's our duty as adventurers to protect the people! H-hey! Aqua! Let go already! Or else—"

Megumin and Darkness kept glancing at me as they talked.

""—you('ll/will) end up like that,'" they finished together.

Aqua fearfully turned to look at me.

"I guess I don't want that... But why not do something about that worthless lump before worrying about me?" Despite her conflicted expression, her words were blunt and rude.

"Hey, you three. I'm pretty good-natured, but I'll only put up with so much. Where do you get off calling a guy 'like that' and 'worthless lump' and whatever?"

"If you don't like it, start by coming out of there," Aqua shot back, still clinging to the sofa.

I had no intention of doing something so stupid, not when it was this freaking cold, so I just burrowed down further.

Under the blanket of Japan's ultimate anti-chill weapon, the heated *kotatsu* table.

We'd gotten back to town after defeating Vanir, general of the Demon King's army.

There, we found the demon perfectly alive and working in Wiz's shop. He'd made a grim prediction for Darkness and talked to me about the best ways to make some money.

Specifically, the plan involved large-scale sales of items from my original world. I would develop the goods, and he would handle mass production and distribution.

I'd been considering the venture myself for a while, and it seemed like easy cash, so at Vanir's suggestion, I was going to spend the idle winter days coming up with products, but...

"...Kazuma, enough is enough. Get out of there already. You are setting a bad example for Aqua. We know how smart you are, and we acknowledge the superiority of the heating devices of your land. But the snow will be melting outside soon. Is it not time to resume our activities?"

I had become a complete *kotatsu* potato. Megumin was bending toward me with a gentle smile and a tone that suggested she was talking to a selfish child.

"She's right, Kazuma. I agree we were greatly indebted to your '*kotatsu*' over the winter. But surely things are better now. Come on, work with me again, like you did in that dungeon. Let's…"

Darkness was wearing the same expression as Megumin. Slowly, they reached out for the blanket keeping in the warmth under my *kotatsu*…

I targeted the defenseless nape of Darkness's neck and intoned:

"*Freeze!*"

"Eyow!" She yelped at the unexpected blast of ice running down her back.

Maybe ice magic really was stronger this time of the year, because Darkness collapsed onto the blanket, rubbing her neck and shivering.

"H-he's fighting back! Kazuma, that is enough already! I know we're not in debt anymore, but lazy is lazy! Come on—we're going! Hey, what are you doing with that hand? No more resisting. Just come with uuuusssss!"

As Megumin reached out to drag me from the *kotatsu*, I simply grabbed her hand and applied Drain Touch.

She screamed and batted at my hand as I absorbed her HP and MP.

In her haste to scramble away, Megumin ended up doing a backward somersault on the carpet.

So there was Darkness, still holding her neck and shivering, and Megumin, pressing her hands to her head where she must have bumped it during her tumble. I said to them sotto voce:

"Don't underestimate me. I know what you take me for, but I've contended with infamous bounties and Demon King's generals and come out on top. You think I can't handle a lackadaisical Crusader and a quasi-Arch-wizard? Go get some levels and try again."

By now, only my head was poking out from under the table.

"…Looks like Kazuma's made himself a force to be reckoned with, with all his little skills. Personally, I don't care if he never comes out of there. Then I don't have to fight anyone for my special spot in front of the fire," Aqua informed the others from the sofa.

They both stood up with tears beading in their eyes and shot venomous glances at me.

Well, they could look at me however they liked. I wasn't in the mood to cave to anybody right now.

In this cold, I wasn't about to go—

Uh-oh.

"Guys, I'm in trouble. This is an emergency. I need to go to the bathroom, like, really bad. I know it's a lot to ask, but how about we call a quick truce? I need you two to grab the mat under the *kotatsu* and carry it over to the toilet."

I cast some magic on the heating element under the table with me as I talked. That was how it generated warmth. If I got out from under the blanket, the flow of MP would stop while I was away, meaning my warm pocket would start to cool off.

Happily, since I had just drained some magic from Megumin, I was in no danger of running out.

I had assumed the two of them would be angry, but they simply exchanged a glance and then, to my surprise, did exactly as I asked.

Megumin grabbed the front end of the mat under my haven. "Take the other side, please. We will throw this man outside, *kotatsu* and all."

"Sounds good. Aqua, I know you don't want to leave the fire, but could you give us a hand here? Just open the door for us."

"S-stoppit! Don't you have an ounce of sympathy for your fellow man?! Hey, stop—! If you take another step, I'll use Steal on you! I'll do it!"

I had discovered that no other skill intimidated women so much.

But Megumin merely sniffed at my threats.

"Have we not already shared a bath together? What could you steal that could possibly embarrass me now? More to the point, if you deliberately steal my panties, I presume you will well and truly be known as a lover of 'jailbait.'"

S-so the worm has turned!

Where did she find the nerve? When did she get so sure of herself?

"Y-you've seen me naked, too. I've even washed your back. So I'm not afraid of any S— Any St— Errgh..." Darkness tried to imitate Megumin's show of defiance but seemed considerably less confident.

"All right! Let's take this worthless *hikikomori* lump and dump him outside!"

"Stop! Wait! W-we can talk! I-I've got it! When it gets a little warmer, I'll help you do two explosions a day! I'll use Drain Touch to take Aqua's MP, and you'll get one extra blast every day!"

That got a twitch out of Megumin, but Aqua had some objections.

"No way! Why should I share my precious, sacred MP for something stupid like that? I'll have you know that my magic comes from the profound faith of my Axis Church followers. They're *my* followers, and this is *my* magic! If you think I'm going to let you use Drain Touch on me again...!"

"You can just ignore her. I promise I'll get you that magic!"

"Ohhh... Two explosions a day... Two explosions..."

"Ohhh... Steal... Steal... No! There's always a chance he might *not* get my panties on the first try..."

Aqua was whining, and Megumin and Darkness were fretting to themselves. Just another morning.

"Mr. Satou! Mr. Satou, are you there?!"

Suddenly, a furious pounding sounded at our door.

2

Who was it but Sena, the prosecutor who had dubbed me a criminal and even gone so far as to take me to trial.

"Mr. Satou, this is terrible! There are Lizard Runners outside town…and…"

She burst in, her face pale, but she sounded less pleased by the moment when she spotted me buried under the *kotatsu* with only my head sticking out.

It wasn't long before her panicked tone had reverted to the one she had used when she was trying to wring a confession out of me.

"May I ask what exactly you're doing…?"

"I believe it's obvious. I'm staying warm on a cold day. Oh, speaking of which, could you close the door?"

Sena heaved a sigh and complied.

"…Mr. Satou. You've defeated no less than two of the Demon King's generals and even brought down a major bounty head. I hold a rather high opinion of you, and I do respect you, but…"

Gosh, I don't like where this is going. All because I wanted to keep warm in my *kotatsu*.

"You can safely ignore him. You must have had some reason for showing up here in such a hurry," Darkness said.

"Oh, that's right! Monsters called Lizard Runners are swarming the area at this moment. Every adventurer in town is trying to get rid of them. Normally, they're not terribly dangerous, but…it seems enough of them were in heat at once to produce a Lizard Runner princess!"

According to Sena, every year around this time, the "Lizard Runners" had their mating season. These monsters were bipedal herbivores who normally posed no real threat to anyone. But the moment a large female known as a "Princess Runner" was born, the creatures immediately became a menace.

Princess Runners gathered more and more Lizard Runners to themselves until a fight to mate with the Princess broke out within the herd.

And the way they fought was very unique…

—They sprinted.

Short distances, incredible speeds.

They were like those frilled lizards everyone used to be so into.

And they didn't test themselves against other members of their own species. Instead, they'd seek out fleet-footed members of other species and challenge them to races. And leave them in the dust, of course.

The lizard that won the most challenges would get to mate with the Princess and become the King Runner, the leader of the whole herd.

Granted, you could quibble about the nomenclature. Like, if the guy becomes a King Runner, why isn't the female called a Queen Runner? But I think the real loser in that argument would be whoever even bothered to engage in the conversation.

Hearing about these bizarre life-forms was enough to make me sick of this world all over again, but to people who rode on horses and dragons and birds, this problem had everything to do with them.

These normally placid Lizard Runners were going to want challengers, and when they did, they would fearlessly approach whatever they intended to challenge—be it a horse or a dragon—and give it a kick to get it going. Then they would set off as fast as they could.

Lizard Runners had a powerful kick, capable of breaking bones and worse.

And now that a Princess Runner had appeared, the Guild was very interested in thinning out the herd as quickly as possible…

"And that's why I'm here, Mr. Satou!"

Sena was gleefully grinning at me.

…Not that I had any idea why. "I'm afraid I still don't really understand your reasoning. The Guild already put out a quest, right? Why come to me personally? Someone will take care of it."

"What are you talking about, Mr. Satou? As I recall, when we were faced with a dungeon, home to one of the Demon King's generals, you said, 'We have to protect the people of the town. That's an adventurer's duty.'"

D-did I say something that cool? …Come to think of it, I guess I did.

"Good luck getting that NEET to do anything. Now that he's paid off his debt and wallowing in cash, I don't think he's even going to move till he needs money again," Aqua called, not sparing me a glance from her place by the fire. "Well, Kazuma does have the lowest level of any of us. I don't blame him for being scared."

She didn't have to add that…

"Hey, since when do I have the lowest level? Aqua, you're… Well, okay, I know your level's pretty high after taking out all those undead. But Megumin's…"

"Level 26."

Megumin showed me her Adventurer's Card with a triumphant look.

"…When did that happen?"

"I eliminated both Destroyer and the Demon King's general Vanir. Not to mention I am often the one who must clean up lesser monsters. Naturally, my level was eventually going to go up."

Seriously?

And with such a high level, she must have gained a fair number of skill points. But I was sure she had just dumped them all into skills that would boost the power of her Explosion spell.

But there was still one person whose level was lower than mine.

"What about Darkness? Her attacks never hit, so that must make it hard to gain levels. I'm sure you don't need me to come out and personally deal with your Lizard Runners or whatever. We should let Darkness go farm some experience…"

"Heh," Darkness snorted.

Then, with no small amount of pride, she shoved her card under my nose.

"You might recall that I was almost solely responsible for getting rid of Vanir's magical dolls. And they gave experience in proportion to the danger they would pose to a normal person…!"

She sounded tremendously proud of herself.

Her card showed her level was 20.

I felt a flash of anger toward the grinning Darkness.

"Ptoo."

"What?!"

She yelped as I spat square on her card.

I ignored Darkness as she tearfully scrubbed at the card. I crawled out from under the *kotatsu* and took out my own card.

Next to LEVEL, it read 13.

…What was I going to do? When had this happened?

And this when, according to Aqua and the others, the weak Adventurer class was supposed to gain levels faster than advanced classes…

Sena cocked her head quizzically as I stared at my card. She took in my expression with her guileless, straightforward gaze…

"What is your level, Mr. Satou? I assume it must be fairly impressive, given you've tangled with the Demon King's generals…"

"H-hey, guys, get your stuff together and let's go on a quest!"

A bit desperately, I cut Sena off before she could say anything else.

3

"Kazuma, you do not seem to get along very well with Sena. Did she subject you to a brutal interrogation while you were in jail?"

Megumin and I were headed to see the blacksmith in town.

I walked along without an ounce of enthusiasm.

"It wasn't brutal, exactly, and I'm not sure I'd say we don't get along. She just…seems to see me as some sort of do-gooder. Personally, I'd just like to live as soft and sedentary a life as possible, so I wish she'd stop looking at me like I'm gonna save the world."

Sena had started asking me for help because I had defeated the Demon King's general Vanir.

But I didn't have some special ability like Mitsurugi. And except for my Luck, my stats were all below average, even for an Adventurer. The only reason I'd defeated any generals or bounty heads was basically just being in the right place at the right time.

And yet she kept coming to me with problems…

"I actually agree with that prosecutor in having a high opinion of you, Kazuma. You have managed to pull out some rather improbable victories against some very powerful foes."

"Are you praising me or making fun of me?"

I didn't get to find out, because we had arrived at the blacksmith's.

The truth was, I hadn't been completely indolent all winter. I had learned some new skills to help me develop the products Vanir and I were working on.

For example, I had asked the owner of this shop to teach me the Smith skill. That made me better not only at working with metals but at all kinds of manufacturing.

It was just that after I created the *kotatsu*, my other work screeched to a halt.

In exchange for teaching me Smith, I had imparted to the blacksmith the process for making a Japanese katana—even if it was just a dim recollection of something I saw on TV once.

Since my cheap short sword was starting to wear out, and since I had come into a small fortune, I decided to ask the shop owner to upgrade my equipment. I promised to buy the first katana he produced.

Also, I knew I could hardly go forever with just a breastplate, gloves, and greaves, so I'd asked him to make me a set of real armor.

I'd been sequestered in the house for so long that I was sure it was just about done…

"Hey, man! You finished? Is my sword just about done?"

"Welcome… Oh, it's you. The sword you taught me to make, that 'katana' or whatever you called it? It's done, as far as it goes. I made it in the shape you described, but…"

The shopkeeper brought out a blade in a sheath.

It definitely looked like a Japanese-style sword.

I took it in hand and drew it out…

"Whoa… You sure got the right idea…! It's not quite as pretty as the real thing, and it doesn't look very sharp, but hey, it'll do."

"Well, excuse me, Mr. I-Wanted-a-Perfect-Sword! I tried to find out about this tempering process you talked about, but I'll be damned if it made a lick of sense to me. I guess it was an interesting enough job. All I have to do now is write the name on this magical tag and stick it to the scabbard, and it'll be finished. This sword is going to be your faithful companion. Better give it a good, strong name," the shopkeeper said with a flash of his teeth as he brought out my suit of armor.

Name the sword, huh…?

I examined the shining blade and remembered the names swords always have in video games.

"Kazuma! Kazuma! Hurry up and give it a name—I want to go explode something! We have been cooped up all winter, and I'm feeling very repressed!"

"You went out to do an explosion every single day. Anyway, hang on. It's a big deal, naming a weapon. You have to give it the attention it's due…"

I settled Megumin down and lapsed into thought.

Muramasa… Masamune… Kotetsu…

"Here you go, the full plate mail you ordered. It's reinforced with Adamantite here and there—top-notch stuff by local standards. Take good care of it."

As I was thinking, the shopkeeper brought out my armor.

The full-body armor, shining blue, made for an intimidating sight. This would definitely protect me from damage.

I gleefully tried it on…

"What do you think? Perfect fit, huh?"

The shopkeeper sounded pleased. And it did fit well, but…

"…It's so heavy I can't move."

"……Is… Is it, now…?"

The smith eyed me with pity.

With my abysmal stats, I apparently couldn't even equip the high-class item I'd ordered.

Luckily, I'm about average size, so the shopkeeper was willing to take the item back, and I didn't have to pay for armor I couldn't use.

I had been hoping to see some serious improvements in my attack and defense, but it didn't work out the way I'd hoped.

I would have to be satisfied with a new weapon.

"So now all that's left is the name... Gotta put my whole heart into this... Kikuichimonji... Kogarasumaru..."

As I stood there with my arms folded, deep in contemplation, Megumin suddenly suggested, "Chunchunmaru."

"...What did you say?"

"Chunchunmaru. That is the name of your sword."

The sword that, for some reason, Megumin was now clutching to her chest.

Nuh-uh. No way.

"I can't give my sword some random name like that. This is a special-order item I worked hard to get. My faithful weapon! It needs an awesome name so that—"

"Hey!" the shopkeeper said, looking at the blade in Megumin's grasp.

I followed his eyes to the magical tag affixed to the scabbard.

The characters on the tag...

"...The young lady's already inscribed the name..."

"Indeed I have. From this day forth, this blade shall be known as Chunchunmaru! Now, Kazuma, I believe your business here is finished. Come, explosions await!"

"Wh-wh-what have you done?! Aww... My sword...!"

With my weirdly named sword in her hand, Megumin dragged me out of the shop.

"—You know, I spent a pretty good chunk of money on that sword... What if I defeat the Demon King with it? There'll be a plaque in a museum somewhere: *Chunchunmaru, Holy Blade of the Legendary Hero.* Do you even understand what you've done?"

Legendary Blade Chunchunmaru

"I gave a bold and arresting name to this sword while you stood there dithering. What are you so upset about? I'm more concerned about whether Darkness has succeeded in convincing Aqua." Megumin seemed just a bit uneasy as she spoke.

Before the two of us had set off to procure my weapon, we had asked Darkness to work on Aqua...

"Noooo! I don't wanna go today! Tomorrow! If tomorrow's warm, then we'll go out! I have a bad feeling about today! Goddess's intuition!"

"Enough with this goddess nonsense! Look, you can't cling to that sofa forev— Ow! Let go of my hair!"

When we got home, we found Aqua and Darkness embroiled in a fight.

I guess Darkness hadn't managed to persuade her... Well, heck.

"Sounds like she really doesn't want to do this one, Darkness. How about we leave Aqua at home this time? The three of us should be plenty."

"There you have it! Every once in a blue moon, Kazuma says something sensible! You heard the man, Darkness, now get your hands off me!"

Aqua started smacking at Darkness's hands, emboldened by what she took as my show of support.

"Anyway, you two, this is our first quest in a while. When we get the reward money, I'll take you out to eat somewhere. We can celebrate with a nice hot pot or something."

I had made the proposal offhandedly, but I noticed the goddess of celebrations perk up her ears.

The other two seemed to have picked up on what I was thinking and exchanged a glance.

"Kazuma is right. Winter is ending, and this is our first day back at adventuring. We will have to have something truly luxurious to recoup our strength."

"Yeah, let's enjoy ourselves today. I know a place that caters to the nobility. I can make a reservation there."

They immediately set about adding fuel to the fire.

Darkness released Aqua's collar, but the goddess anxiously interjected, "You… You know, you could buy the ingredients, and we could all have a hot-pot party at home. Tell you what. I'll even make all the preparations so it will be ready when you come home exhausted from your adventure. We can have a little party here at the house."

She gazed up at us, still glued to the couch.

We looked at her.

""""Take care of the place while we're gone,"""" we chorused.

"Waaaaaah! I'm sorry! Don't leave meeee!"

4

Pockets of snow still speckled the field outside town.

"All right, we've got a good position. Let's get started!"

I was perched in one of the few trees around the area, ready to do some long-distance sniper work with my Deadeye skill. I gave the signal.

"Cool, I'm good anytime! This is a great way to get your piddling level to go up a bit. And the sooner you get strong, the sooner you can defeat that Demon King for me."

Aqua stood beneath the tree I was positioned in, arms crossed, glaring at my intended target.

Come to think of it, I guess I *was* supposed to defeat the Demon King at some point…

"Yeah, with Aqua's buffs in place, we could take on a whole herd of these things!"

Darkness planted her feet there with her great sword plunged into the earth, her hands resting boldly on the hilt. She formed the picture of bravery.

"If any get through, leave them to me. When they are near, I shall blow them all away at once."

Megumin gripped her staff calmly, a smile on her face.

Everyone but me is above level 20 now, and our equipment is up to snuff. We're more or less intermediate adventurers now.

"All right, here we go, then! Just like we planned. I'll start by sniping the King Runner and Princess Runner. Without them, the Lizard Runner herd ought to break up, and we can mop up the small fries. If my shooting doesn't do the trick and they attack, I'll hit them again while Darkness keeps them busy. If *that* doesn't work, Megumin will use Explosion before we get surrounded, and I'll pick off any survivors. Aqua's on support… Okay, ready?"

Uncharacteristically, our plan today accounted for the possibility that something might go wrong.

Just more proof that we weren't amateurs anymore.

From my perch, I used my Second Sight skill to get a bead on the distant Lizard Runner herd.

They looked just as Sena had described them. They were reptiles resembling huge, green, bipedal frilled lizards.

One of the Runners was twice the size of any of the others. It had a horn on its head like a crest and appeared to be giving orders to the other creatures.

"Hey, Aqua, you see the one with the horn? I know that's the Princess, but which one's the King?"

"How should I know? Maybe it's the one that looks the most dignified?"

I wanted to ask her how I was supposed to recognize a dignified lizard, but it was my fault for asking her anything in the first place.

The Princess Runner had that distinctive horn, but how could I determine which one had won the running competition?

That was when I realized the Princess was always close to one particular lizard.

Of course. The winner becomes her mate.

So the one she was the friendliest with had to be the King.

I set my sights on him and drew my bow all the way back...

"I've got it! Leave it to me, Kazuma; I have an idea. The King is the one who won the running competition, right? So he's got to be the fastest runner here! One of my holy magic spells attracts monsters—it's part of a pair with the spell that repels them. I'll use it to summon the Runners, and the one that gets to me first must be the King!"

Except I'd wanted to know which one was the King exactly so I could shoot him from a safe distance. Her suggestion was the most backward thing I'd ever heard.

"*What* are you talking about? Do goddesses stick their hands in a fire just to see if it's hot? I already have a guess which one's the King, so don't do anything stu—"

"*False Fire!*"

Aqua was chanting before I could stop her. A pale-blue flame appeared in her hand. I wasn't a monster, but the sight of it still made me want to jump down and punch her in the face.

The impulse came mainly from the magical power, but I admit, it was partially because she had gone and done something stupid.

The Lizard Runners seemed to have caught sight of the flame, too. With a bizarre screeching sound, they came running straight at Aqua.

""""Geez!"""" Darkness, Megumin, and I all exclaimed, taken aback by just how quick the Runners were.

Megumin hurriedly began chanting Explosion, but at this rate, the monsters would be on Aqua long before she finished.

Darkness stood in front of Megumin, while I held my bow and shouted at Aqua, "You dumb idiot! You're never happy until you've done something to screw us over, are you?! Stick to party tricks from now on! We could've taken out the King and Princess nice and quiet, and none of these guys would have been any trouble! And you had to go and stir them up!"

"Wh-what are you so angry about? I was doing my best to help—don't get upset at me! Fine, I get it! I know how this is gonna go! I'm sure those Runners will do something awful to me, and I'll end up in tears. I know my part—now, are you going to kill them or just hang there?!"

Defiant in her anger, she went from looking desperate to flinging herself spread-eagled on the ground to sulk.

"You moron!" I shouted. "At least make with the support and healing! Don't just lie there; they'll trample you, and you really will die!"

At the same time, I took aim at the King Runner, who was barreling toward us at a terrifying speed, and let loose with my Deadeye skill.

My aim was true. I hit the creature at the front of the pack right between the eyes.

Success with Deadeye was partially based on your Luck stat. I had hardly handled a bow in my life, but with the skill and my Luck, I made a decent archer.

I had assumed the death of their king would be a serious blow to the lizards' morale. But for some reason, they just picked up speed.

"Hey, Aqua, naptime's over! I took out the King, but it's only made them go faster!"

Aqua was still laid out with her eyes closed, her head turned away.

"If you get rid of the King, it just means a chance for one of the other males to take over. You have to take out the Princess first!"

"You couldn't have told me that one dead lizard sooner?! M-Megumin! Megumiiin! Is your magic ready to go?! Use Explosion! There's plenty of space! Take them out in one fell swoop!"

"Leave it to me! Wah-ha-ha-ha! Taste my combustive magic! *Explosion*!!!"

Nothing happened.

"?! Oh no! My MP! Kazuma, I don't have enough magic to ignite the explosion!"

"What?! Why now, of all—? Oh crap!"

I had absorbed some of Megumin's magic with Drain Touch that morning!

"Wh-wh-what do we do, Kazuma? The Princess! The Princess Runner is really running…!"

I looked up. Perhaps enraged by the death of her partner, the Princess Runner—a massive lizard with a frill around her neck—had joined her entourage in dashing straight for us.

Aqua was flopped on the ground just beneath the tree I was in, and Megumin was next to her.

Darkness moved out in front to protect them…

"Fwa-ha-ha-ha-ha! Have at meee!"

She sounded awfully excited. Downright thrilled, in fact.

And then the crowd of Lizard Runners broke against her like a wave.

"Yaaaah! K-Kazuma! Dear Kazuma!"

Now Aqua was shouting for me.

The Princess Runner seemed to be glaring straight at me, as though she knew I was the one she wanted. Given how quickly she was approaching, she was probably about to just jump and kick me right out of my tree. Man, was I in trouble!

"D-Darkness! Just hold them off a little longer! I'm going to take her out!"

"T-take your time! Yaaagh! No r-rushhhowww!"

Darkness spoke through the hail of kicks the Lizard Runners were administering below.

I drew my bow and aimed at the Princess's brow, just below her frill.

"Kukieeee!"

"Deadeye!"

As she launched herself up at me with an animal screech, I fired down at her.

At point-blank range like this, it would have been hard to miss even without my skill.

The arrow buried itself in the Princess's forehead, and her flying kick ran out of steam before it reached me.

"That was a close one…!" I muttered, breaking out in a cold sweat.

Then I felt the impact.

The corpse of the giant Runner had collided smack against the trunk of the tree.

I was defenseless, since I was trying to both shoot and look cool at the same time, and I went tumbling out of the branches.

The lizards below watched my descent.

—I fell right past them.

I landed headfirst on the ground, a dull *crack* sounding in my ears.

"K-Kazuma?! Are you all right?! Aqua! I don't think Kazuma's supposed to bend that way! Healing magic, quick…"

Megumin's pleading voice rang in my ears as my consciousness dimmed…

5

"………"

"………"

I stared vacantly ahead—face-to-face with the goddess Eris.

We were in the same sanctuary-like room I had found myself in after my death at the hands of General Winter.

I'd arrived there just as suddenly.

Before me was Eris with her long silver hair and blue eyes, as inhumanly beautiful as the last time I'd seen her.

This was a real goddess. And she was tapping her lip with a finger, apparently very troubled.

"…Um, could you try to take a little more care with your life? I bent the rules for you and let you be revived last time, and you wouldn't believe the trouble I got in… I'm sure your friend, my senior goddess, is going to browbeat me into releasing again, but I'm the one who has to deal with the consequences…"

"I'm sorry. There's nothing I can say this time. I'm very sorry!"

I fell out of a tree and died as I was celebrating my victory over the Princess Runner. I had to admit it was a pretty ignominious way to go.

Eris heaved a deep sigh.

"I understand there are occupational hazards involved in adventuring work. But…you just weren't paying enough attention this time…"

I bowed my head to her.

I was sure she was right: Aqua would resurrect me soon enough.

And Eris would have to take the heat again.

"Umm… What happened to everyone after I died? Are they okay?"

"Yes, they're fine. I don't know what exactly my senior goddess was doing on the ground like that, but the lizards trampled and kicked her until she started to weep for help. Darkness held the enemy off long enough for the herd to break up after the Princess Runner fell. Miss Megumin is safe, too, thanks to Darkness's protection. My senior is tending to your body now."

Thank goodness. At least we succeeded in driving off the lizards.

I could afford to just hang out here for a while, then.

I wondered if I'd received a massive blow to the head and lost consciousness immediately, or if I was just used to this by now.

For someone who had just died, I found myself strangely calm. I scanned my surroundings, taking everything in.

"…You seem relaxed about your death this time. Usually, people are rather distraught when they come here."

"Well, between Japan and this new world, this is my third visit."

My eyes swept the room as I spoke to her.

…It's really empty.

Eris silently watched me goggle.

There wasn't much to do, and we found ourselves staring at each other.

…What to do? This is super awkward.

Stupid Aqua. What's taking her so long?

But…

"Don't you ever get bored, standing by yourself in an empty room? I don't know what the population is in your world, but is it enough to keep you busy?"

Eris's smile remained in place as she answered. "That's a good question. I'm responsible for people who lose their lives by monster, so I usually have plenty to do. But in winter, when all the adventurers stay inside, I'm happy to say I have lots of free time. If I'm bored, that means everyone is alive and well. Nothing makes me happier than having time on my hands."

My lady Eris smiled wider as she spoke.

Oh man. This is trouble. My chest is getting tight, and my face is getting hot…

…Ah. I see. I'd always thought something was missing from my life in this new world.

Here I lived in a house with three women, but where were the sparks?

I admit, none of them were exactly bad-looking. And yet…

I had the self-proclaimed goddess who spent all day napping in front of the fire, eating, and napping again. The stubborn Explosion nut who just turned fourteen the other day who could get me sent to prison. And the "Young Lady" with a great body accompanied by a parentage and proclivities that were nothing but trouble.

Sheer hotness wasn't what I truly wanted, you see.

I wanted a woman with a little sense, someone kind and caring.

—Yes! Here's my female lead.

Or so I was thinking as I stood there red-faced and flustered.

"But you know, I don't spend all my time here. Sometimes I get someone to cover for me and go down to have a little fun on the mortal plane… That's another of our little secrets, okay?"

She gave me that mischievous wink and laughed.

S-sure…

I nodded at her, still blushing.

Kazuma! Kazuma, can you hear me? I cast Resurrection. You can come back anytime. Just have Eris open a gate for you.

I heard her, all right. I heard her yet again completely failing to discern that I was having a moment.

Couldn't she have given me just a tiny little bit more time?

I found myself experiencing the exact opposite feeling from a few minutes earlier. I clicked my tongue.

"I'll catch up with you in a bit. I want to keep chatting with Milady Eris here. Just keep an eye on my body, okay?" I shouted into thin air.

I wasn't sure if she had heard me or not, because there was a moment of silence. Then:

Huh?! What are you blathering about? Stop being dumb and get back here already so we can raise your level, bump off the Demon King, and get me back to Heaven!

Aqua's words dragged me back to reality.

The Demon King.

Right. We'd come here to slay him. And here I was, few levels and no power.

And saddled with a veritable brood of problem children, each with her own unique and frustrating quirks.

Even if I came back to life, wouldn't I just spend the rest of it trying to defeat the Demon King with those three?

Yeah. I saw the reality all too well.

What was I expecting? That if I worked hard enough, I would suddenly discover some mysterious power within myself and conveniently wipe out the final boss? Not likely.

If anything, I figured there were plenty more visits to this little room in my future.

And what would I get for all that work?

I didn't answer Aqua but stood there, musing.

I considered the life—and all its hardships—that most likely waited for me.

I decided to be reborn and start a new life instead.

"Hey, Aqua! I've decided I'm tired of that life! I'm not coming back. I'm gonna take a do-over as a baby somewhere. Give everyone my best, okay?"

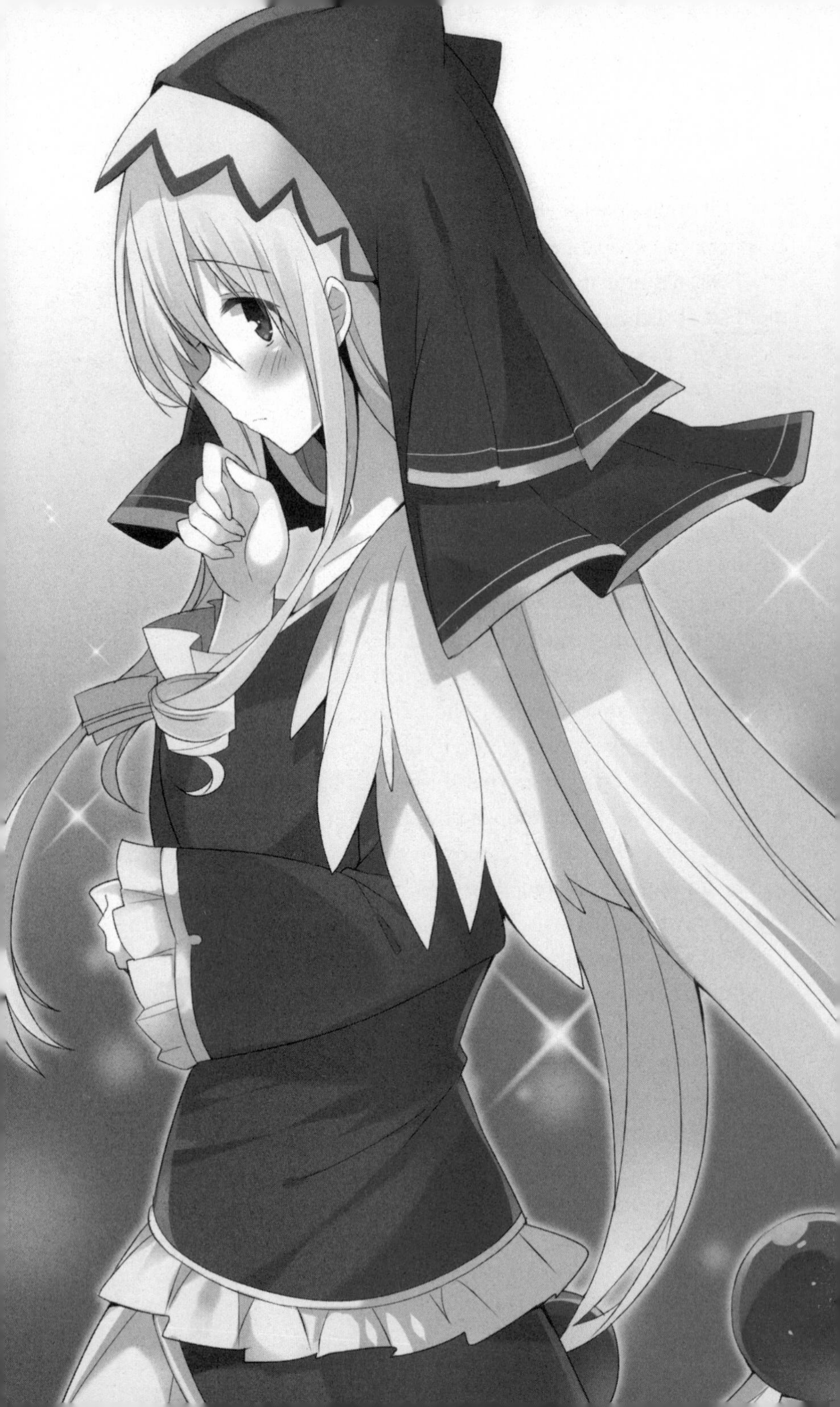

"What?" Eris yelped with surprise at my words.

Eventually…

What is this nonsense?! J-just you wait a second!

I turned to Eris as Aqua's voice grew increasingly frantic.

"You got that? Sorry to trouble you, milady. If it's possible, could you…make sure I'm a guy in my next life, too? And that I'm born into a house with a gorgeous older stepsister and an adorable younger one?"

"Hold— I mean— Just— Wait a moment!" Eris was as startled as Aqua.

Then I heard Aqua's voice again:

Kazuma! Darkness says that if you don't get back here posthaste, she's going to scribble all over your face! She's got a marker, and she looks awfully eager…

A-as if that would change my mind. I mean, I'm dead. What do I care what they do with my body…?

…? Megumin, what are you doing? Those are Kazuma's clothes— Megumin?! H-hold on!

"Hey, quit it. What are you doing to my body? Don't you disrespect the dead! I'm gonna give you the haunting of your life!"

What *was* she doing to my earthly remains?

I was mulling it over with mounting anxiety when Aqua cried:

Megumin! Megumin!! Wai— Kazuma, dear Kazuma! Come quick! Get back here right now!

"Well, stop her! Aqua, whatever Megumin's doing, why don't you stop—? E-Eris, milady, could you open that gate for me? Please!"

Eris giggled at my panic and snapped her fingers. Before the sound had faded, a white doorway stood before me.

I got to my feet, ready to dive through it…

"Now then, Mr. Kazuma, I'll be praying for you to stay safely in the physical world from now on. Have a nice trip!"

And I pulled open the door…

6

The first thing I saw was Megumin, her face flushed red in apparent anger.

She was crouched over my prone body, pressing out wrinkles in my shirt at my chest.

"Hey, what are you doing? Here I thought you were the one sensible person here, other than your name and your fixation on explosions! I'm dead for five minutes, and I find you doing this?"

Megumin stood without a word about what she had been up to.

"What? If you have a problem with my name, let me hear it! This is all because of your ridiculous joke about not coming back. The next time you say something so outrageous, I'll do even worse to you."

A ridiculous joke? She'd probably get really pissed if I told her I'd been more than half-serious.

I got to my feet, too, checking over my body.

"Seriously, what did you do to me? Is it going to make me embarrassed to ever see you again?"

I glanced at Darkness, who was covering her face with both hands and blushing up to her ears.

I looked questioningly at Aqua, who had been crouched there waiting for me to come back to life, but…

"What, you want me to profane my holy mouth with that? Ask the culprit."

And she pointedly turned away from me.

"Okay, Megumin, tell me already. Otherwise I'm gonna be super awkward around you…"

"You'll figure it out when you go home and get in the bath… I'm more worried about your head. Are you all right? Not feeling sick at all?"

I felt around my head and neck, but everything seemed normal.

Oh right. I had died by falling out of a tree.

"Your neck was in awful shape, Kazuma," Aqua said. "At first I thought you were pretending to be that girl from *The Exorcist*. It was a serious enough wound; I prescribe avoiding combat for two weeks."

I flinched. *The Exorcist*. Wasn't that the movie where the girl turned her head around backward? Had I done that?

Megumin patted me on the shoulder as I clutched at my neck, pale and trembling.

"You should hurry home and rest for today. Look. Thanks to you, the Lizard Runner herd broke up. Good work. I shall report on their defeat, so you go home."

Gee, she was acting awfully nice now. Maybe she was worried that the shock of dying had gotten to me.

After gratefully accepting her show of kindness, I collected Darkness, who still wouldn't meet my eyes, and Aqua, who was occupied with comparing her feet with the footprints of the Lizard Runners, and made for our mansion.

When we got to town, Megumin set off for the Adventurers Guild, and the rest of us headed home.

"Hey, Kazuma. I was wondering—what made you say such dumb stuff, anyway? You're living an easy life surrounded by beautiful women. What could possibly make you so unhappy that you wouldn't want to come back?"

Darkness nodded vehemently in agreement with Aqua.

I just looked at them. "…Pfft."

""Hey!""

They responded to my snort with a chorus of surprise.

We reached our house, and I was just about to open the door when Aqua started in on me.

"Hey, don't you think you haven't been treating us very well lately? Like today. I worked hard to bring you back to life, even if you didn't want to come back. So stop treating me like some kid you want to get rid of! You should worship me properly! If we go to Arcanletia, the city of water and hot springs, you'll see statues of me and branded merchandise and everything! It's amazing!"

I wondered what kind of people made branded merchandise based on their pantheon. I didn't even turn around as I replied, "Idiot, when have I ever treated you like I want to get rid of you? Without you around, who would clean the bathroom? Isn't that the perfect job for someone who claims to be the goddess of water?"

"About that! I'm the goddess of water, not toilets! That's exactly what's so awful about how you treat me! You should value me more!"

I just ignored Aqua as she stood there crying and annoying me with her complaints. I entered the house, removing my chest plate right in the foyer.

Darkness came in, shedding her armor, which was covered in lizard footprints.

She seemed unable to stop sneaking peeks at my lower body.

...?

Mystified, I glanced back at her, and she quickly averted her eyes.

Of course I wondered what was going on, but I was a little sluggish, having just returned from the dead.

I wanted to hurry up and get some rest, so I went to take the first bath.

In the bathing area, I set my hand on the magic-powered heating device and turned it on. I entered the changing room, stripped off my clothes, and...

...came flying right back out.

"Where's Megumin?! Is she back yet?! I hope she doesn't think I'll go easy on her just because she's a kid! I'll keep Stealing from her until she knows exactly how I feel!"

"Megumin said when she was done at the Guild she was going to go stay with a friend for a few daaaahh!"

Darkness, relaxing on the sofa with a magazine, raised her head to find me naked as a jaybird and quickly buried her face back in her reading.

I still had no idea what her criteria for embarrassment were, but today I didn't have time to wonder.

Aqua looked at me, my eyes bloodshot and my teeth clenched, and said, "......Hey, Kazuma. I'm glad you're so comfortable with yourself, but don't you think that's kind of boastful?"

"Y-you idiot! Megumin wrote this! You were *there* when she did it! Aww, damn it alllll!"

I fled back into the bath.

Half in tears, I scrubbed at the words Megumin had scrawled on my waist: *Legendary Sword Excalibur ↓.*

Chapter 2

May There Be an Invitation for This Brazen Layabout!

1

I sat on the sofa as a meek-looking Megumin pleaded with me.

"I apologize for the other day, so please, go back to being your usual self, Kazuma!"

She bowed her head, kneeling formally on the carpet. I was sprawled on the couch wearing a fuzzy robe.

We had been like this ever since Megumin had returned from her friend's place.

The other day...?

Oh, she means when she scrawled all over my *parts*.

"Such a minor thing wouldn't trouble me anymore. They say the rich don't bother to fight. Won't you have some tea, Megumin? We've got some very high-quality leaves."

I smiled at her as I spoke.

Megumin appeared ready to burst into tears, perhaps overcome by my show of magnanimousness.

"I am so sorry, truly! I was wrong—so *please* return to the Kazuma I know! This performance is disgusting! Please! I beg you!!"

"What's all this nonsense about going back to my usual self? I've always been this way."

I smirked, basking in the heat of the fire. Aqua held out a teacup to me with an elegant gesture.

"I made a cup of the finest black tea, Kazuma, my friend," she said, cradling her own cup as she sat down beside me.

I took a sip of the fresh tea...

"...This is just hot water."

"Oh my. What a silly thing I've done. I'm sorry, dear Kazuma."

"No worries. You can just try again. Thank you, Aqua. I'm happy with this."

"What is *wrong* with you?! What happened while I was out of the house?! I am begging you! Will you both not return to your right minds?!"

I instructed Megumin to calm down as Aqua went to make more tea.

She must have accidentally turned the tea into plain water while she was preparing it.

But I was feeling as beatific as the Buddha and was hardly going to get upset over something like that.

Darkness beckoned Megumin, who was now utterly confused.

The Arch-wizard approached with a weary expression, and Darkness proceeded to explain the events of the last several days...

2

It was the morning of the day after Megumin had made her escape.

"Curse that jailbait scum! The minute she shows her face around here again, I'll skin her alive! I swear I will! I'll make that self-righteous squirt beg for mercy!"

I was hopping mad. Darkness, her face flushing slightly, said, "I-if you do that, Kazuma, the cycle will just continue. But, uh, tell me more about how you plan to make her beg for mercy..."

We were in the living room. I was doing all my shouting from under the *kotatsu*, while Darkness sat next to me, hugging her knees and inquiring with great interest.

From her place in front of the fire, Aqua said to us, "It's too early for all this noise. Gosh, all you ever do is fight. You should learn to be a bit mellower, like me. Except for my bath, I haven't moved from this spot since we got home yesterday."

"Yeah! You've eaten there, you've slept there—that's not what I would call mellow. More like lazy! Damn it alllll! Once that stuff dried, it was almost impossible to get off! I'll never forgive her! I can see her weeping, pleading face now!"

"So, uh, tell me more about this weeping and pleading..."

In the middle of all this, we heard a knock at the door.

"Megumin?! Is that you? Have you come crawling back?!"

"Tell... Tell me more..."

I crawled out from under the *kotatsu* and stormed toward the door.

"Bwa-ha-ha-ha-ha-ha! Did you think I was a strange-minded girl of the Crimson Magic Clan? I am sorry to disappoint, but it is I! My dear shopkeeper is brilliant enough to know that she herself has no idea how to tell a winning innovation from a pile of rubbish, so she has enlisted me, a demon with highly regarded powers of discernment, to come and talk business on her behalf. Good fortune will come if you fall on your face in joy and gratitude for my visit! Now, show me what it is you intend to display at our shop! ...Hrm?"

A suspicious-looking masked demon greeted me.

Aqua rose unsteadily off the couch at the sight of him.

"Hey, hold on. How'd you get in here? I put a holy barrier around this house exactly so slime like you couldn't get anywhere near us!"

"Ah, that bothersome trifle? Was that supposed to be a barrier? It was so weak, I assumed some novice priest put it up mistakenly. Oh, and please pardon me. It seems I shattered it merely by passing through it."

Aqua was now standing smack in front of Vanir.

"Goodness gracious, did you know parts of your body are missing here and there, O powerful demon? And here I'd heard that you were the Duke of Hell or something. Surely such an exalted personage wouldn't be reduced to such a state just because of my paltry barrier."

With an innocent smile, she began to poke interestedly at the damaged bits of Vanir's form.

"Bwa-ha-ha-ha-ha! Well, this body is simply a bit of earth. I have plenty more where this came from. I was just curious about that veil around this house. For the work of a village neophyte, I'd say it wasn't bad. A *human*! Bwa-ha-ha-ha-ha!"

Vanir laughed merrily, but Aqua furrowed her brow in anger and got up in his face like some two-bit gangster trying to be intimidating. Vanir stared evenly back at her.

"H-hey, this looks bad. Darkness, help me break these two up...! ...What are you doing over there? Why are you ignoring me?"

"...No reason."

Maybe she was sulking because I had ignored whatever she was trying to ask me earlier.

Darkness was sitting in the *kotatsu* with her back to me, paying no attention to the commotion at the door.

"Hey, you two. I know you want to fight, but we're indoors here. Take it easy." With no other options, I tried to worm in between them. At least they each took a step back.

"Hey, Kazuma. I don't really get what's going on here, but is that *kotatsu* or whatever the thing you're going to sell? Don't tell me you're going to do business with this slime! Are you seriously going to sign a contract with this parasite on mankind, this insect who feeds off negative emotions and only ever thinks about how to upset the humans around him so he can steal their souls? What an awful joke! Pfft-hee-hee-hee!"

"Bwa-ha-ha-ha-ha, we demons find contracts an annoyance. We prefer to work on the basis of trust. And not the kind practiced by those deceitful groups who attract the gullible with talk of 'just trusting God' and then take all their money in the form of 'tithes.' What was that pitch, again...? Oh yes: *God is always watching over you*, wasn't that it? You know, I think I saw that in practice just the other day. That man they arrested for 'watching over' baths and toilets a little too closely— was *he* God? Bwa-ha-ha-ha-ha-ha-ha!"

Both of them laughed uproariously, and then…

"".........""

…suddenly fell silent.

"*Sacred Exorcism*!"

"Brilliantly dodged!"

At Aqua's shout, a pillar of light appeared at Vanir's feet, but he immediately tossed his mask aside. The light swallowed and destroyed his former body, but his true form, the mask, neatly avoided the demon-quelling magic.

Another body bubbled up under the mask right away, despite the fact that it had landed on the carpet.

Aqua launched herself not at the developing body, but at the mask, and tried to rip it off the body's face. "Ah-ha-ha-ha-ha-ha! So this is it! This is your true form, right?! I've got you now! There's no getting away! The only question is what to do with you!"

"Bwa-ha-ha-ha, even if you destroyed this mask, there would soon be another and another for me! H-hey, stop trying to take my mask off while I'm talking! My mouth will disappear along with the rest of me! At least wait until I'm done trying to…"

"Okay, enough already. Calm down, you guys." I stepped once more between Aqua, who was gleefully trying to tear off the mask, and Vanir, who was less than gleefully trying to fight back.

Vanir was sitting on the carpet and inspecting several of the items I'd made.

"Mm. It seems my judgment of you was correct, boy. These are quite marketable. I'm sure they will sell. And this—*kotatsu*, did you call it? What a fine way to stay warm."

"…" Darkness, sitting under said device, slapped away Vanir's hand as it explored the blanket covering the table.

I still didn't know what she was pouting about, but I hoped she wouldn't interfere with business.

"All right then, let's talk terms. Currently, our agreement is that we will pay you one tenth of the profits on the items each month. But perhaps you would be interested in selling the actual intellectual property rights to these devices, boy? I would give you…three hundred million eris for all of them together."

""""*Three hundred million?*""""" we all exclaimed in unison. Vanir was eyeing with particular interest a rubber object I'd produced.

Three hundred million…! That was enough money to never have to work another day in your life, assuming you didn't overindulge.

Before we had recovered from our shock, Vanir kept talking.

"Or you could take the monthly profits. Either is fine with me. With something like this, I think as soon as we can set up a means of production, we'll be looking at more than a hundred thousand eris in sales every month. We can wait to settle the details until we're ready to sell it… Incidentally, what is it for?"

A hundred thousand a month, or three hundred million in a lump sum.

Uh-oh. I was about to start playing the game of life on easy mode.

There were no guarantees it would keep selling forever, so maybe I should just take the lump sum?

Or, no, maybe I should take the monthly amount. Then I wouldn't have to worry if my savings started to dwindle.

But now that I thought about it, it was this demon who was going to do the selling. Couldn't he get arrested wandering around town in that mask?

"It's called a balloon. It's a toy that expands when you fill it with air. Give it here."

Aqua took the rubber object from Vanir and began to blow it up.

"Ooh, let me have one." Even Darkness showed an interest, putting one of the balloons to her lips.

…I guess it was too late to tell them that it was for contraception, and that it had been awfully hard to make it thin but durable.

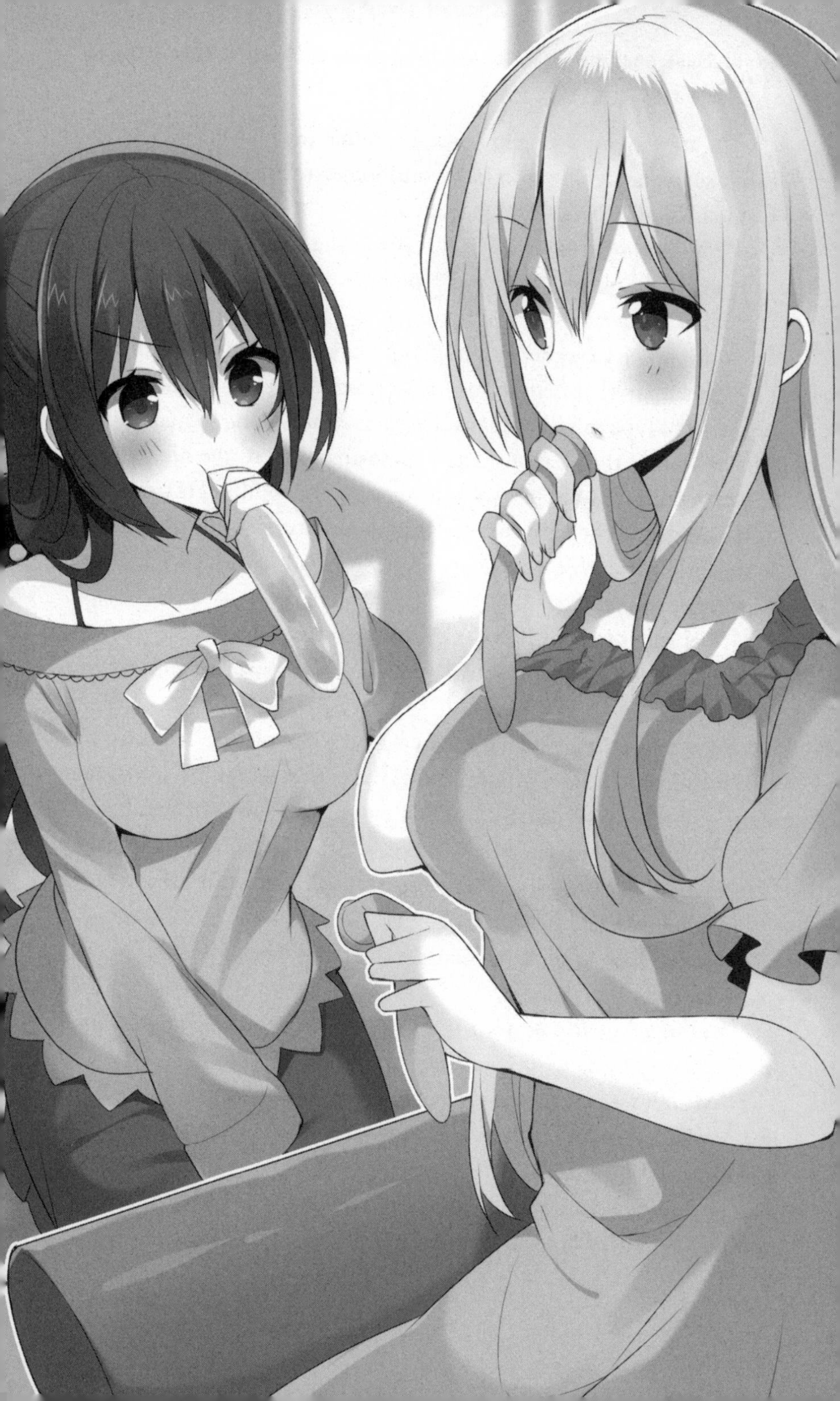

"A-anyway, are you going to walk around town like that? Don't you think someone's going to notice you? Someone might be like, 'It's the Demon King's general!' and attack you."

"? What nonsense is this? This is not the mask I had before. Can you not see the glowing numeral *II* on it?"

What about it?

I was going to argue with him, but Darkness gestured me over.

"Kazuma. That demon may have a deeply flawed personality, but he's not the type to kill humans. He's not even helping to maintain the barrier around the Demon King's castle anymore, so the higher-ups at the Adventurers Guild just want to keep an eye on him. He's staying at Wiz's shop, and she used to be a famous adventurer. I'm sure she could handle him if anything came up," she whispered to me as I worked my way under the *kotatsu*.

I got it. As long as he wasn't causing any serious trouble, they figured that rather than antagonize him, it was smarter just to leave him alone.

However outrageous he might be, this demon was still a former general of the Demon King's army. There was no telling how much destruction he could cause if he got it into his head to turn hostile.

"So from a bureaucratic perspective, the Demon King's general Vanir is defeated and gone. They won't even ask us to return the reward."

Well, I was glad to hear *that*.

I would hate to get mired in debt again just when I was on the cusp of becoming a rich man.

…You know, it'd be great if you could give me your serious explanation without playing with a condom like a balloon.

"Mm. It will take some time until we're ready to sell. You can let us know which form of payment you prefer later. Now, I am worried about the shop, so I must be going."

"I think you should. Or my pure, holy house is going to stink of demon. Get out of here. Go on, get!"

Vanir left, grinding his teeth, with Aqua making shooing motions behind him.

—*Man, a hundred thousand a month or three hundred million at once...*

3

"...And they've been like this ever since."

"I see. Now I understand why they are putting on such airs," Megumin said, glancing at me as Darkness concluded her explanation.

Incidentally, my beloved *kotatsu* had gone with Vanir.

I had expected to go back to fighting with Aqua for a place in front of the fire, but apparently, a fat wallet makes for a big heart.

Aqua and I were both seated on the sofa together, perfectly friendly. Megumin eyed us for a moment with some exasperation and then finally stood.

"Well, I'm certainly glad we have money. And that we can rest assured that we will have no trouble with resources in the future... Very well, let us go defeat something! Kazuma, you have more levels to gain!"

She lifted her staff high and smiled brightly.

"Huh? What are you talking about? I just got a huge windfall, and you think *now* I should work? Forget my level. Who needs it?" I said curtly as I sipped the second cup of water Aqua had brought me.

...You know, it would be nice if one of these cups contained actual tea at some point.

"...Wha...?"

Megumin seemed put out.

"Look," I said, "last time, we had equipment, we had a plan, and I still wound up dead. I've decided. No more defeating anything for me. I'm going to make my living as a merchant from now on. I'll have a nice, easy life with no dangerous adventuring work."

"Umm, Kazuma...friend, I'm kind of with Megumin on this one. Don't we have to get rid of the Demon King?"

...Hmm.

"Then let's earn even more money and hire a bunch of powerful adventurers. They can help me raise my level and even lend a hand in taking out the Demon King. That's the strategy. We attack the Demon King's castle with an army of high-level adventurers. What do you think? Can't you just taste it?"

"That's perfect! You're full of good ideas. We'll ride those adventurers' coattails right to the gates of the Demon King's castle, then when he's weakened, you can strike the final blow!"

"Exactly. It's obvious you've known me longer than anyone else here—you know just how I think."

As Aqua and I sat there grinning at each other, Megumin was visibly trembling.

"Y-you would defeat the Demon King with the power of money? No! I will not have it! What do you think the Demon King represents? He is a great and terrible enemy whom you confront with your friends after pouring your heart and soul into raising your level to discover the power hidden within yourself or whatever, and whom you finally defeat in a climactic ultimate battle! And you would send hired thugs after him?!"

"Look, that sounds great and all, but be realistic. You really think it would help to raise my level? I'm pretty sure I could get all the levels I wanted, along with lots of nice equipment, and His Majesty could still snuff me out in a single attack. So instead, once we've taken care of enough of his generals to bring down the barrier around the castle, we get some high-level Thieves to sneak in with Ambush..."

"What an untoward tactic! Worthy of the enemy himself! Darkness, say something to them! They get worse and worse every d— Darkness?"

Darkness seemed to come back to herself with a start.

"Oh, I...I was just wondering, if you let Kazuma just go on getting more and more corrupt, just how scummy do you think he'd become...?

He'd never work, just sit around drinking, and pretty soon he'd become profligate with his money... Eventually, he'd say to me, 'Hey, Darkness! Go do whatever you have to do to get us some money!' And then I'd start selling myself, convinced that one day Kazuma would have a change of heart..."

"You are getting worse, too! Oh, what am I to do?!"

"Don't lump me in with that perv, Megumin. You might remember I just died recently. Lizard Runners? Broken neck? At least leave me alone until I've recuperated a bit."

"You fell out of a tree. Yes, you need rest, but I fixed you up so well that there shouldn't be a scar or any pain," Aqua interjected from beside me. I ignored her, pointedly rubbing my neck.

"...I understand," Megumin muttered, looking down.

"You do? Great. In that case, I'm going to go take a nap—try to help this injury heal and get back to the field of battle, you know? Oh, and could somebody wake me up later? I'm going out with Dust and the guys for a drink."

I started making for my room even as I spoke.

"...I understand. Let us go to heal your wound," Megumin said, still staring at the floor.

"*Go* to heal it? It'll be fine if I just hang around here for a while."

"A good bath will bring your strength back even quicker. Let us go to Arcanletia, the city of water and hot springs."

"You know what, forget my injuries. What did you just say?"

I was sure I had just heard her say something like *hot springs*.

Let me stress how important this was.

I had just heard the words *hot springs*.

"Hot springs?! Did you just say Arcanletia? Did you say we're going to Arcanletia, the city of water and hot springs?!"

Aqua seemed even more excited than I was.

I guess it only made sense. She did claim to be the goddess of water.

And speaking of hot springs...

Speaking of hot springs...

"H-hot springs... You're right. We're all tired after so many difficult battles. And we're not in debt anymore, so why not treat ourselves sometimes?"

"What's with the monotone, dear Kazuma?" Aqua was staring at me from inches away, my face illuminated by the fire.

I wish she would stop looking at me so intently and from such a short distance.

Suddenly, I thought I could sense Megumin's downcast eyes gleaming.

"May I take it the two of you agree with this plan, then?"

I couldn't see her expression, but I thought I could catch a hint of a sinister smile...

"And Darkness...?"

"—And when I've finally fallen as low as I can go, I'll say, 'Don't leave me! I—I will do anything, Masterrrrr!'"

She was completely lost in her own little world, blushing furiously and writhing around. Megumin stiffened.

"...She could stay here and watch the house," I said.

"...W-well, but without Darkness, we may get in trouble on the road," Megumin said with a hint of reluctance.

On the road...?

4

The next morning:

"Rise and shine! Come on, how late are you gonna sleep?! Is everyone ready to go? Wake up! Wake up! Come on!"

Aqua's shouting reached every corner of the house despite the early hour. She must have been awfully excited about our trip to roll out of bed this early.

As for me...

"Of course I'm ready! Gosh, and those two call me human trash. Are they ever going to get up?"

"Totally! I'll go get them up and at 'em. You go to the carriage station and reserve the best seats."

"I'm on it. Actually, there's somewhere else I'd like to drop by first…"

Trusting a slightly puzzled Aqua to wake the others, I gathered up our bags and left the house.

Arcanletia, the water and hot-springs capital.

It was about a day and a half's carriage ride from Axel Town. If you got the first carriage out in the morning, you'd only have to camp once.

We didn't know yet how long we were going to be gone, and I wanted to let my business partners know we would be out of town.

I went in the door of the cozy little magic item shop, which opened early each morning.

"Welcome to— My, my. It's the nocturnal boy who keeps the waking hours of the undead. What brings you here so early? If you've come to talk to the owner, she is within, albeit a bit tanned by my heat ray."

Inside the shop, Vanir was hastily stuffing something into a box. Farther in, I could see a scorched Wiz lying on the ground.

"…Isn't she your employer? Can you get away with that?"

"Naturally. If I let this know-nothing owner do as she liked, we would be stuck in the red even after a thousand years of work from me. As soon as I take my eyes off her, she's ordering absurd stock that throws off all my profit calculations."

I was exceedingly curious about what had happened, but my business today was not with Wiz but with Vanir.

"I've actually come to see you today. I've decided to go on a little hot-springs vacation. Can our business discussions go on hold until I get back?"

"Oh, I see. We still don't have a plan in place for production, so please, take your time. Best wishes that you'll get to enjoy a mixed bath."

"M-m-m-mixed bath?! No way! We're just going for my health—to help my neck! ...Anyway, what are you putting in that box? And why is Wiz all...charred?"

Vanir showed me what he was trying to pack away.

"Our half-baked proprietor brought this to me in a tizzy just moments ago. As I recall, her exact words were: 'This is a wonderful item! It will sell for sure! No question! So, Mr. Vanir, please get out of your death-ray stance... Please...?' I was going to simply send it back, but...do you want it?"

"...? What is it? Some kind of magical item?"

"Allegedly, a solution to the perennial adventurer problem of how to deal with bathroom business while in the field. It's a magically compressed toilet that constructs itself the moment you open the box. It even makes the sound of flowing water for privacy."

"Awesome. That sounds really convenient."

After all, bathroom needs were a serious issue for adventurers, whose work often kept them outdoors overnight.

"Its drawbacks, such as they are, are that the flushing noise is loud enough to attract monsters, and the mechanism that creates the water is too powerful and has a tendency to flood the immediate area."

"I-I'll pass, thanks. Any other magic items you recommend?"

In response, Vanir took a potion bottle from the shelf.

"A recommendation, is it? How about a potion that explodes when you open it, which our penurious proprietor stocks for reasons I cannot fathom? They cost three hundred thousand eris each, but imagine how much you could make if you took one to the bank and threatened to open it in front of one of the tellers. How about it?"

"Not for me. Aren't there any useful items in this shop?"

At that, Vanir heaved a sigh.

"Our senseless shop owner has a singular talent for stocking items that cannot possibly be of any use. If I so much as take my eyes off her, she starts ordering things I've barely even heard of…"

But then he stopped.

"…Oh yes. Boy, you said you were going on a hot-springs vacation?"

"…? Sure, but…so what?"

Vanir flitted nearer to me.

"Perhaps you could take my senseless shopkeeper with you. I'm going to need some capital to start production on your items, but with her around, who can say what bizarre trinket she'll waste our resources on next? This girl's a much better Lich than she is a businesswoman. I see all, yet even I cannot judge the outcome if there were to be a power struggle between the two of us."

"…Are you telling me to take Wiz for her own protection? I mean, I don't mind, but Aqua *hates* the undead…"

"For such a slender shopkeeper, she has a surprising preference for large baths. Receive this prophecy from me, the all-seeing demon: At your destination, there shall be an opportunity for mixed bathing."

"Leave it to me! I'll be careful with her."

When I got to the meeting place by the carriages, Aqua and the others were already there.

"I thought I told you to go ahead and save us some seats. Hey, what's that on your back?"

It was, in fact, Wiz—blackened, unconscious, her eyes rolled up in her head. I explained my discussion with Vanir.

"Huh? Fine, I guess," Aqua said with surprising calmness, "but did you notice she's starting to fade a little?"

She was right. Wiz was looking a little more transparent than usual.

"Oh no! Is she okay?! Quick, healing magic—I mean, no! Not on an undead!"

"Calm yourself, Kazuma," Megumin said. "Now is the time for Drain Touch. Use it to transfer some vitality to her!"

"Going out of town…," Darkness murmured. "The last time I did that was when I was a girl and Father took me to the Capital for the princess's birthday… Hmm? Kazuma? What are you doing, taking my haaaaand?!"

I grasped the Crusader's hand as she sat there lost in her own little world and Drain Touched her.

I transferred the vitality I took from her into Wiz, who started turning a bit more solid and finally opened her eyes.

"Huh…? Mr. Kazuma, is that you? Where are we…?"

Darkness was busy wringing my neck as Wiz scanned her environs in confusion.

"D-d-drain *me*, will you?! Here I was finally enjoying some old memories! Why is it always an ambush with you?!"

"Hrrrgh, what else could I do? It was an emergency! You've got more HP than anyone else here, right?!"

"Sir and ladies! If you don't get aboard, we're going to leave without you!"

5

As adventurers, we might have been able to get ourselves hired as guards, but I wasn't actually keen to do any battles, on the off chance something did happen. So we just paid the fare like everyone else and traveled as simple passengers.

I didn't want to fight.

I had been killed just dealing with some of the weak monsters right near town. What chance did I stand against anything big enough to want to attack a crowded carriage?

Luckily, the reward from our battle with Vanir had been almost ten million for each of us.

We were finally taking a vacation. Why not enjoy ourselves a little?

*   *   *

"Hey, Kazuma! Let's take that carriage! I can tell it'll be the smoothest ride! I call the window, by the way. Be sure to pick seats where we can get a good view of the scenery. Come on, Kazuma, go buy our tickets. Hurry up, you don't want everyone else to get all the good spots."

Leave it to Aqua to set her heart on the most expensive-looking ride available.

It was a smallish carriage; the driver's seat and the passenger area were joined, with room for luggage at the back.

And the luggage rack already had plenty of luggage on it.

The wooden passenger seats behind the driver should have had room for five people, but…

"…Hey, mister, why is one seat already taken? What's this? It's kind of in the way…," I said.

One of the five places was already taken.

And not by a person. A small cage sat there with a lizard inside.

It was about the size of a cat, with red eyes that had a nasty glimmer.

No. It couldn't be…

"That, sir, is a baby Red Dragon. Its owner is riding in the other carriage, but they paid for the dragon to have a seat in this one. I'm afraid someone in your party is going to have to ride with the bags. Although I know it won't be comfortable…"

"I see," I said, accepting the explanation.

So this carriage would be cheaper by the price of one ticket. We wouldn't want to ride with just one stranger, so I decided to stick with this one.

"So the only question is, who rides in the back—?"

"Let's play rock, paper, scissors!" Aqua interrupted me. "I think that's the best way to decide these things."

Apparently, she was starting to learn that she always drew the short straw when it came to things like this. Maybe she had sensed that somehow she would end up with the luggage if she didn't do something.

"U-um, I know you weren't expecting me to come along, so how about I take that spot?"

Wiz was raising her hand hesitantly. I had explained that we were bringing her along at Vanir's insistence.

But Vanir had already given me money to cover her travel expenses.

We couldn't do something so unfair to one of our number.

"No, Wiz, we're going to play it fair here. Rock, paper, scissors it is, Aqua. I don't mind."

"Huh?" Aqua seemed thoroughly nonplussed by my quick, sure answer.

…Rock, paper, scissors? I was in.

I hadn't realized it existed in this world, too.

I guess the Japanese guys who got here before me must have spread the good word.

Darkness and Megumin didn't object, either, but just got ready to play.

With a shout, Aqua made a fist…

"Okay then, here I go! Rock, paper, scissors!"

I pulled scissors while everyone else had paper. I won this round.

I made to board the carriage, but Aqua stopped me.

"Who said we were doing it elimination-style? All five of us play together, and we keep going until there's one loser."

"You're kidding."

I should have known there was something funny going on when she brought it up.

…Fine.

"Okay, Aqua. How about you and I go one-on-one? Three rounds. If you win even one of them, I'll sit with the luggage."

"No way, seriously? You must be even stupider than you look. Don't you even know about probability? The chances of you winning three times in a row are, like, nothing."

I simply faced her down, gesturing to the other three to get on board.

"I've never lost a game of rock, paper, scissors."

Three rounds. Rock, paper—!

"—No way! This makes no sense! You must have cheated! Come on, one more time! If I lose *this* time, I'll sit in the back for real!"

Aqua, half in tears, kept accusing me of suspicious behavior. She sure could be persistent when she wanted to.

"For real? If you keep pestering me after this, I swear I'll tie you down there with a rope."

Aqua gave a confident little chuckle at that.

"You're on. I don't know how you're cheating, Kazuma, but if that's how you want to play, I've got a few tricks of my own! *Blessing*!"

"Hey! That's playing dirty!"

Aqua had cast a buff on herself that bestowed the luck of the gods. The exact effects varied from case to case, but basically, it raised your Luck stat for a while.

"They say luck is a kind of ability—well, my magical ability is a kind of luck! Now, here we go! Rock, paper—scissors!"

I won again.

"But howww?" Aqua whined as I made a shooing motion toward the luggage rack.

"It's weird, but I've never lost a game of rock, paper, scissors, ever since I was a kid."

It was the only case in which I believed in my allegedly excellent Luck.

"You're awful! That's cheating! You were basically born with a special ability! So you don't need my blessings—just send me home! Right back to Heaven, you damn cheater!"

This goddess!

"You dumb jerk! Are you saying my unique special ability is playing rock, paper, scissors? How stupid are you? How is that supposed to help me survive around here? Do I just walk into the Demon King's castle and tell him, 'Hey, how about if I beat you at a children's game, you stop bothering everyone'?"

"But— But—!"

As Aqua stood there, still protesting, I finally just grabbed her.

"But you know what ticks me off the most? That you think you're a blessing! That's the stupidest thing I've ever heard! What's a blessing about you? If I could send you back and get an actual special ability instead, you'd be in Heaven so fast—!"

"Waaaah! How can you say that, Kazuma?! Hey, thoppit! Leggo ob by cheeks!"

6

I lost track of how long we'd been traveling in the rumbling, rattling carriage.

Our hometown was completely out of sight, and we were surrounded by unfamiliar countryside.

There was a small window mounted in the side of the carriage, and having never been very far outside town, I was watching the scenery roll by. Even though I was supposedly an adventurer, this was the first chance I'd had since coming to this world to travel and really take in what was around me.

Darkness was sitting next to me in full armor, glued to the window, watching the world go by with the wonder and curiosity of a child. Since she was the daughter of a noble house, maybe it was her first time outside the area, too.

Only Megumin was more interested in the cage with the dragon in it than she was in the sights beyond the window, perhaps because she'd had more experience of the outside world than we had.

I thought I heard her mutter something about Chomusuke being cuter, but she must have wanted to feed the creature anyway, because she had stuck a hand in her pocket and started fumbling around to see if she had anything to give it.

Then there was Wiz, who was smiling and petting the strangely affectionate Chomusuke on her lap.

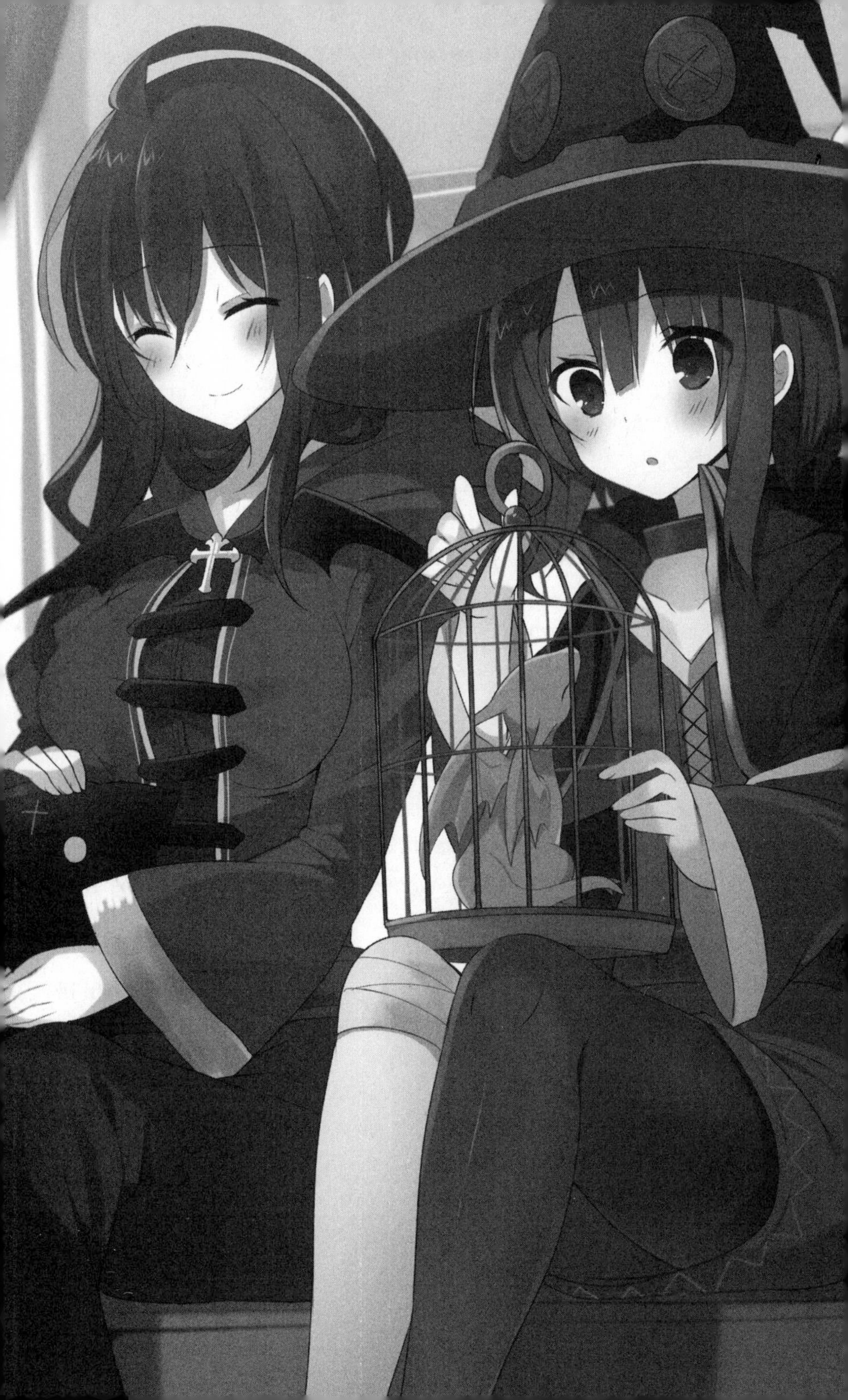

—An altogether quiet ride. Until…

"Kazumaaaa! Dear Kazumaaaaa! My butt hurts! A lot! Could somebody trade places with me soon?"

Aqua called back to us from the lurching luggage rack.

Sheesh, all right.

"Fine, I'll switch with you at the next rest stop, so just hang in there till then."

Aqua was overjoyed at that and began humming happily among the cargo, hugging her knees to her chest.

"Are you sure you don't want me to change with her?" Wiz asked. "I wonder why Mr. Vanir said I should go on this trip, anyway. Hee-hee… He's been so thoughtful to me. 'Wiz!' he'd say. 'You just sit at the counter grinning. No need for you to do any work.' So thoughtful…"

She related this to us with a smile.

I hadn't told her the real reason Vanir had asked us to bring her along. How could I?

"Huh," Aqua said, "who knew that masked weirdo could be so nice? Are you sure he's not planning something?"

"Aqua, milady, Mr. Vanir does have his good side. Lately, he's been chasing away the crows that flock the local trash pile. All the women in town call him Vanir the Crow Slayer."

What is a demon doing just hanging around the neighborhood, anyway?

Our carriage was part of a whole caravan of vehicles stretching down the road. They carried travelers, adventurers hired as bodyguards by the merchants, and all kinds of cargo.

A large contingent of people and carriages meant weaker monsters were likely to keep their distance. With a group this size, we would probably be fine.

That was what I kept telling myself, anyway.

Even though I knew perfectly well by now how this worthless world worked.

*   *   *

—I was the first to notice it, too.

Since my Second Sight skill was active as I gazed out the window, I spotted a cloud of dust in the distance.

And it was headed straight toward the road we were traveling on.

It was still a ways off, but it was getting bigger and bigger at a rate that suggested its source was moving at a pretty good clip.

"Hey, what's that?" I indicated the cloud to Darkness, who had been busy looking through the other window. But without the Second Sight skill, it seemed she couldn't make out the dust cloud, and she only looked at me in confusion.

As an ominous sense started creeping over me, I called to the driver.

"Excuse me, there's some kind of dust cloud coming this way. Pretty quickly, too. Do you know what it is?"

The driver had an easy grip on the reins. He replied:

"A dust cloud? Moving fast? Around here, the only thing that would account for that would be a herd of Lizard Runners. But word is the Princess of the Runner herd was taken down just the other day, so maybe it's a Sand Whale blowing out some sand. The only other thing I can think it might be is Dashing Hawkites."

I'm not a big fan of monsters with bad puns for names.

"Heh, don't look at me like that. I didn't come up with the name. It's a kingly avian, a crossbreed of a hawk and a kite. It can't fly, so instead it runs at high speeds using its powerful legs. When it finds prey, it leaps on it. Very dangerous creature."

I would really prefer not to be attacked by a monster with such a stupid name.

The coachman must have been able to tell what I was thinking, because he chuckled and said, "It's all right, sir. Spring is their mating season, just like the Lizard Runners. To attract the attention of the females, the male birds put on a display of courage called a chicken race. It's very strange. They pick something hard, something that would be very unpleasant to run into, and then they sprint straight at it, only dodging away from it at the last second. Apparently, some overzealous birds actually collide with the object and die. But they generally seek out tough, durable things. I'm sure they're just over there flinging themselves at trees or rocks or something."

I see. That's reassuring.

Satisfied, I returned to my seat.

But when I looked at the cloud of dust again…

It's even closer.

There was no mistaking. It was nearer than it had been before.

And it was clearly headed straight for us.

"Excuse me. Excuse me! I swear it's coming this way, and fast. Are you sure we're all right?"

At my words, the driver tugged on the reins, slowing the horses in an attempt to get a good look at the oncoming haze.

"…Ah, that's certainly some Dashing Hawkites. No question about it. But why would they be coming toward us? I wonder if the merchant carriages have anything exceptionally hard in them, like Adamantite. Those birds do love tough substances. The merchant caravan seems to have noticed them. Don't worry about… Hmm? They… They do seem to be coming this way. They… They seem to be coming for *this* carriage…!"

They were definitely headed directly for the passenger seats of our vehicle.

Meaning…!

"Kazuma! Some extremely fast animals are approaching! I think… They're focused on me! Wh-what intense stares! *Pant…pant…* Th-this is bad, Kazuma, very bad! I'm afraid they're going to run right over me and trample me into the ground…!"

"You?!" I had the sudden urge to grab my head with my hands.

"I'll stop the carriage, ma'am! The adventurers riding in the other vehicles will dismount and protect you—and us!"

…Gee. Sorry our Crusader is so tough.

I whispered to Darkness, "Hey, Darkness, those monsters are after you. They like running into hard objects. They want those rock-hard muscles of yours."

"Kazuma, I do have some shred of womanliness. Don't describe my muscles as rock-hard. Anyway, my armor is a special-order item with just a bit of Adamantite in it. And with my defensive skills... I'm sure that's what's drawing them... N-no, seriously. Stop looking at me like that. My body isn't *that* tough...!"

The carriage came to a halt, and Darkness and I got ready to jump out of it.

"Megumin, Aqua, we're up! I know we didn't want to fight, but we brought these guys on the caravan, so we'll clean up our own mess."

At that, the four of us dismounted.

"I'll help, too!" Wiz called, following us out.

"Vanir trusted me to take care of you," I said. "I know how strong you are, but stay in the carriage for now. Look after the driver!"

Wiz nodded. The coachman, who didn't fully grasp what was going on, shouted, "Sir! We didn't take you on as bodyguards—you paid to come along, so please simply wait somewhere safe!"

I'm sorry, man! I'm pretty sure my party is the cause of this problem!

Not that he could hear my mental apology.

"Adventurers! Come to our aid!"

His voice signaled the adventurers guarding the caravan to leap out of every carriage, weapons in hand.

Darkness began walking straight toward the flock of Dashing Hawkites that were charging us.

I'm embarrassed to say I was making sure to stay safely behind her.

Even if I'd been out front, those monsters would have run right over me.

I had Aqua chanting support magic and Megumin ready to let off Explosion at any time.

The birds coming at us had heads like hawks and bodies like ostriches. They ran faster than a horse and were larger than a cow.

And they showed no sign of slowing down.

"Hey you, Crusader! You're not part of the defense—fall back!" one of the warriors called.

But Darkness kept advancing.

"Look! They're heading straight for her! That's the Decoy skill! That Crusader isn't even one of the hired guards, but she's using Decoy to draw the enemy to her!"

That was one of the archers speaking.

No, actually, she's not using any skill. I'm sorry.

"Wow, that Crusader's not budging a step even with all those enemies coming at her! S-so cool…! So… So brave…!"

This came from a female spell-caster.

I'm sorry. I suspect you've totally misunderstood why she's doing this. I'm so sorry.

As Darkness stood there, blushing and trembling, an adventurer who looked like a Thief boldly came running up behind her with a rope.

"Do you think we can let a regular passenger, someone who paid money to ride with us and isn't even getting a bodyguard fee, put herself in danger on our behalf?! Leave the fighting to us! Take this—*Bind*!"

"What?!"

Darkness reacted instantly to the words.

I recalled Chris telling me about this skill. Bind was a Thief ability. Chris said when she and Darkness had adventured together, she would use this skill on an enemy to keep it from moving, and then Darkness would finish it off.

That explained it.

Hearing the name of the skill, Darkness reacted with speed I'd never seen before from her.

Into the path of the Dashing Hawkites— No, into the path of the Bind skill, as if to protect the oncoming monsters...

Darkness joyfully hurled herself between the man and his target.

She was instantly bound hand and foot by the rope and fell to the ground, where she rolled about like some kind of giant worm.

The thief stared dumbly at her. Blushing, Darkness shouted passionately at him:

"Hrrgh! What is this?! To be captured and bound with the enemy before my very eyes! Now... Now I am sure to be trampled by all those monsters!"

I'm sorry. I am so sorry for our resident pervert.

The monsters raising the cloud of dust kept right on coming at Darkness.

The Thief guy raised a shout.

"I don't believe it! You were afraid that the flock would target me when I used Bind on them—so you took the hit instead?! I am so sorry! Here I was trying to defend you, and instead I just got in the way! Please forgive me!"

No, I'm sorry! I'm sorry for my party members! I'm the one who should be begging for forgiveness!

7

—A game of chicken.

It's where you make a mad dash at a cliff or some other life-threatening object and stop only at the last possible second.

Right now, the object of that game...

"Kazuma! Kazuma, they are upon me! They've come! Now I'm really done for! It's hopeless! Oh, I shall be traaampled!"

…was Darkness, bound hand and foot.

The Dashing Hawkites advanced with their heads lowered, charging Darkness as she writhed on the ground, just about to stampede over her…except they didn't. One did a sort of elegant high-speed backflip over her and then continued on at its furious pace.

The creature moved past me and the other adventurers as easily as the wind itself.

The next one almost ran over her, too, but then it did a forward flip. The next one, a kind of midair split, and the one after that, a barrel roll—each of them leaping over Darkness the instant before they would have made contact.

"Kazuma! Is this some kind of panic play?! This feeling, this last-instant reprieve…! Oh, these males are leaping over my head with such passion…!"

"Will you put a sock in it?! We're in public here!"

Next to me, Aqua had puffed out her chest with a triumphant expression that all but begged for compliments.

"Yeah, fine, nice work," I said. "When we're done here, I'll switch seats with you."

That evoked a fist pump from Aqua.

I had had her cast Blessing on Darkness—a buff that temporarily raises the target's Luck. It would make her chances of not getting stepped on just a little bit better.

While we had been standing there, the adventurer guards had set to work.

"They're too fast for physical attacks! Use magic!"

This prompted a chorus from the spell-casters:

"*Lightning!*"

"*Blade of Wind!*"

"*Fireball!*"

They flung every spell they had at the onrushing monsters.

The creatures that took the magical blows lost consciousness but none of their speed, slamming into carriages and adventurers. Their tremendous velocity meant they were carrying plenty of momentum, and it was going to be hard to stop them.

The people and vehicles that fell victim to the hurtling Hawkites sustained serious damage.

The surviving members of the flock, having all jumped over Darkness, made a sweeping arc without slowing down.

The merchants and adventurers watching them looked shaken: Were they coming back this way?

But I was watching Darkness, still flopping on the ground and still the monsters' target.

And then I got an idea.

I grabbed hold of the driver, who was watching the scene, dumbfounded.

"Hey, mister, are there any cliffs or anything around here?"

We could use Darkness as bait to get the flock to destroy itself.

We would get Darkness right to the edge of the cliff, using a rope or something so she wouldn't fall. Then the Hawkites that jumped over her would find nothing but thin air underneath them…!

"No, nothing quite like that around here… What we do have is a cave you can take shelter in when there's a sudden rainstorm, but not much else."

Well, I thought, listening to him. *Guess you can't always have such a convenient solu—*

A cave?

"Mister, is that cave nearby?! Please get this carriage over to it! Megumin, Aqua, jump on!"

After I'd given these orders, I ran toward Darkness. I started trying to undo the rope around her…

"?! What the hell?! There's no knot! What am I supposed to do with this?!"

There was no way to untie her!

I turned to the guy who had used Bind on Darkness.

"I-I'm sorry!" he said. "That skill keeps the target from moving for as long as it lasts. The only other choice is to cut the cords one by one with a dagger or something…"

You've got to be kidding.

When I turned back to the flock of Hawkites, I found the lead bird almost on top of us. We were out of time!

"Kazuma, I don't know what you're planning, but just drag me along! This rope's tough; it would take forever to cut through it! Don't just stand there—do what you have to do!"

"You're not wrong, but since this is all your fault, I wish you'd shut up!"

The carriage was ready to go, and I headed toward it, dragging Darkness (who was awfully heavy) behind me.

"The Dashing Hawkites are coming for you!" someone warned me.

At the same moment, I heard a series of magical blasts.

With the sound still ringing in my ears, I tried to climb aboard…

"What am I supposed to do now? I can't get in; you're too heavy!"

"What do you mean, *I'm* too heavy?! Have a care—say my *armor* is too heavy! Just tie me to the carriage with the rope or something! We've got no choice; this is an emergency! Come on, just do it!" she insisted, looking awfully fired up about this. *We should call her Dorkness.*

"Hey, if you need some rope, use this! Sorry for all the trouble!"

It was the adventurer who had used Bind on Darkness, throwing a length of rope to me.

I'm the one who should apologize…for our pervert.

I tied Darkness to the carriage…

"Sir, we can't take any more! The carriage will break!" the driver said with a hint of panic.

"Don't worry!" I shouted back. "Just go! Darkness, if it gets too rough back there, just shout! I'll untie you in a hurry!"

Darkness already seemed oblivious to my words, blushing as she struggled against the ropes, apparently in anticipation of what was about to happen to her.

"Ahh… The horse is going to drag me along…! And those starving males are going to chase me…!"

She might actually be happier if I just leave her tied up.

The carriage set off at a furious pace, with Darkness relishing her ride behind it.

"Kazuma, Darkness is—! I always knew you were a monster, but this is beyond the pale!"

"It… It is too much…"

"No! This wasn't my idea! Darkness said…!"

As I sat there in the carriage, enduring the slander of my friends, the driver gave a shout.

"What should we do, sir?! They're coming this way! Right for us! Where should we turn?!"

I suspected he would have been happy to throw us out right then and there, but he had already taken our money and couldn't very well get rid of us now.

"To the cave! Head for that cave we talked about earlier!"

The Dashing Hawkites drew closer and closer behind the fleeing carriage.

They were faster than we were. *Damn. At this rate, they'll catch us…!*

"*Bottomless Swamp!*" A clear voice rang out in the carriage.

At the same moment, a huge swamp appeared between our ride and the oncoming monsters.

The bird at the head of the flock was immediately ensnared and began sinking in the mire.

The owner of the voice was Wiz.

Seeing that we were going to be overtaken, she had wasted no time in casting a spell.

But the rest of the monsters were taking a detour around the morass and setting to catch up again.

The Dashing Hawkites were almost upon us, and as for their target, Darkness…

"Nnggahh! Gods! My armor groans! All that covers me is about to shatter, leaving me in a state unfit for a daughter of nobility…! S-stop! Kazuma, don't look at me—I don't want you to see me debased like this!"

For someone burning red and begging not to be looked at, she sure was enjoying herself.

Once in a while, she found the time to glance back at us, and our collective stare only served to inflame her further.

Well, that was who she really was deep down.

Whatever happened to my cool party member who had been ready to sacrifice herself to take down Vanir?

"*Heal*! *Heal*!"

Next to me, Aqua was frantically casting recovery magic on Darkness.

"Kazuma! I can see the cave! I am prepared to use my magic at any time!"

"Perfect! Wait for my signal!"

Inside the rattling carriage, I gave Megumin her instructions, then pulled out my bow and readied an arrow…

"Driver, you see the cave? Stop the carriage right next to it! Aqua, give me a physical strength buff! …Hrk! *Deadeye*! *Deadeye*! *Deadeye*!"

I turned toward the flock of Dashing Hawkites, leaned out the window, and fired as fast as I could.

Thanks to the skill I was using, most of my shots found their marks, piercing the birds through the head.

Seeing their companions fall, the surviving Hawkites spread their wings and threatened us with high-pitched cries even as they ran.

"Piiiihyorororororororo!"

So that was the "kite" part of "Dashing Hawkite."

While I was feeling rather pleased at having solved this mystery, the coachman gave a shout.

"Sir, we've reached the cave! In dry conditions like this, I guarantee there won't be anyone in there! Do whatever you want to it! …We're going to make a sudden stop—hang on tight!"

Everyone grabbed hold of whatever they could, and the carriage came to a screeching halt just outside the entrance to the cave.

The flock of Hawkites was right behind us.

And unlike us, they made no effort to stop. If anything, they had picked up speed in their anger at being attacked.

—With my physical strength enhanced by Aqua's spell, I jumped out of the carriage, grabbed the rope connecting it to Darkness, swung her around my head as if I were winding up for a hammer throw, and then flung her just in front of the cave.

"Whaaa...?! Not bad! I like where this is going! Leave it to you, Kazuma, to think of something like spinning me around and then hurling me to the mons— Hrk!"

She landed face-first in the dirt at the cave entrance and went quiet.

At the exact same moment...

"Piiihyorororo!"

The Dashing Hawkites zoomed straight toward her, screeching all the while.

They lowered their heads until they were practically on the ground, then dodged inches before they collided with Darkness.

Front flip, backflip. Barrel roll, split.

One after another, they leaped over her, as if of one mind. Straight into the cave.

And at the moment the last one had disappeared into the entrance...

"Megumin! Do it!"

I yanked on Darkness's rope to get her away from the cave as I gave the signal to Megumin, who was all chanted up and ready to go.

"*Explosion*!!"

She loosed her ultimate attack directly into the cave.

A single ray of light flew from her staff, lancing into the darkness as if chasing the monsters that had run into it.

We heard a rumble well up from deep inside.

8

Long after the sun had sunk into the horizon...

Together with the members of the merchant caravan, we had made several large bonfires that served as our campfires.

The carriages were circled up around the fires like a barricade. Not only did this serve as a windbreak while we all camped, but if any monsters should attack, it would give us a modicum of defense, too.

The trade-off was that it wouldn't be easy to get the carriages moving quickly, but that was next to impossible in this darkness, anyway. From that perspective, it was a very practical setup.

"Now, help yourselves! We've roasted all the best parts—dig in!"

The acting leader of the merchant contingent offered us some well-cooked meat.

As the ones who had helped deal with the Dashing Hawkites that afternoon, we were being hailed as heroes.

I figured this was no time to tell them it was our Crusader who had attracted the creatures in the first place. We felt guilty about that, and it led to a little reluctance on our part to engage in the festivities.

"What a display! Who knew there was a mage powerful enough to wield Explosion among our number? Not to mention a venerable Archpriest capable of healing such grave wounds so easily and a gallant Crusader who could face down a flock of Dashing Hawkites without giving an inch! Delaying them with a swamp spell—that's advanced magic! And you, sir—leading them to that cave to dispose of them was a stroke of genius! Truly brilliant!"

Aww, gimme a break...

It's not what you think... It's all our fault...

"Oh, hardly. It was just luck. Really, I keep telling you, we don't need any reward for guarding the caravan..."

"How can you say that? Your party was almost entirely responsible for saving us from the Dashing Hawkites!"

That's right. They wanted to give us a reward for protecting them.

"No, no, really, no. It's really all right! Any adventurer would have jumped in to help in that situation. We don't need it! Seriously!"

I started to get a little panicked as I tried to convince them to drop the subject.

Even I didn't have the nerve to proudly accept a reward for solving a problem I had caused.

But for some reason, the leader of the caravan was absolutely transported with emotion.

"You precious people! You shining specimens of humanity! Oh, to know that in this bitter, cynical world, there are still purehearted adventurers like you!"

…Yeah. Great.

I think I'd better get out of this conversation before he discovers the truth.

Aqua was going around to the other campfires, doing her party tricks and receiving applause and wine in return.

For some reason she even had Wiz with her, dragging her around from one place to the next.

After I'd set her in front of the cave as bait, Darkness had been blown backward by the gust from the explosion, leaving her armor riddled with scratches and dents.

She herself had hardly been injured, and what minor scrapes she got, Aqua had already healed.

Now she was next to me, fixedly watching someone repair her armor.

And the one doing that work was me.

I hadn't expected the smithing skill I picked up for R&D to come in so handy.

Megumin was observing me just as closely as Darkness while I worked. I had no idea what about this was so interesting to them.

To repair the dents, I temporarily removed the shock-absorbing material on the inside of the armor, pounded out the deformities from the inside, then used sandpaper to polish away any scuffs. When all that was done, I laced the cushioning back in...

"You know, it's really hard to work with the two of you staring at me."

At that, Megumin replied, "Oh, I was just thinking what skillful repair work you do. You could probably make a living as a smith if you wanted."

"...Mm. It's exciting, somehow, to watch my own armor being restored."

Both of them had a sparkle in their eyes as they spoke.

There were more than ten carriages in our party and a proportionate number of people. The dozens of us were all camping out under the stars, feasting around bonfires—*this* was a fantasy world as I'd always imagined it.

Suddenly, there was a commotion around the fire where Aqua was showing off her skills.

I looked up. She must have shown them one of her more impressive party tricks.

The crowd was plying her with approbation and calls for an encore.

"Again! Aqua, milady, show us that trick again!"

"We'll pay you! Please do it again!"

The people from the merchant caravan were insistent.

Maybe showmanship was her true calling.

The people in this caravan had come from all over to trade. This was the moment I finally came to accept that they really hadn't heard of my party and its terrible reputation. After all the trouble today, people from our town, the ones who knew us well, might have suspected we were somehow behind everything.

...Phew. I'm getting tired.

Since we weren't hired guards, there was no need for us to take a shift on watch during the night.

I informed the others I was going to sleep.

"...Yes. Sleep well," Megumin said, "but be prepared to get up at any time."

For some reason, she was smiling.

Midnight.

Some kind of sound awoke me. The people on guard didn't seem to have noticed it.

I glanced over at my companions, who were all sleeping soundly by the fire.

Well, I couldn't make out Aqua or Darkness, but Megumin and Wiz were asleep.

So why did I have such a bad feeling?

I heard the noise again, faintly, just beyond the barricade.

Maybe I should wake the others.

"Hey, Megumin, get up. You too, Wiz. Something's wrong."

I shook Megumin's shoulder. But she went on sleeping happily, drool dribbling from the edge of her mouth.

"Megumin! Wiz! Wake up, will you? Wake up, or I'll... I'll do something so embarrassing you won't even be able to look at me for days! Look, I don't care if you don't wake up. It's no problem for me. I had a good reason for trying to get you up. But you wouldn't. So I'm not gonna hold back, okay? Sure you don't want to get up?"

"You think that's an excuse? Just what are you up to?"

"Eeyikes!"

I almost jumped out of my skin at the voice from behind me.

Y-you're gonna give me a heart attack!

"Geez, Darkness, don't scare me like that. If you're awake, then say something. You almost caught me doing something awful."

I had thought she was asleep on the other side of me.

"...I really am curious what you had in mind. But hold that thought...," she whispered, carefully looking around.

What had happened to the disappointment of a Crusader from

this afternoon? The Darkness who was vigilantly scanning the campsite looked like a real adventurer.

…*Huh?*

I felt a twinge. It was my Sense Foe skill kicking in.

The adventurer on guard must have been the Thief from earlier. He probably had the same skill I did, because suddenly he was raising the alarm.

"There's something here! Everyone, wake up!"

Adventurers and merchants alike came leaping to their feet.

I activated my Second Sight skill, peering into the night beyond the carriages. I could discern several squirming human forms.

…Were there…people out there? They seemed to be moving a little too sluggishly for that.

"Whatever they are, there's a bunch of them! Humanoid forms, but moving slowly!" I called out, and the guards picked up long sticks, igniting the ends in the fires to illuminate the area around the camp.

Writhing in the torchlight were…

…terrifying figures, shedding patches of rotten flesh.

Zombies: major undead.

""""Ahhhhhhh!"""""

The flickering light made the image especially horrifying, and everyone who saw them started screaming… Myself included, of course.

Darkness was standing there with her great sword in hand, although she didn't have her armor on.

I indicated Megumin, who was still fast asleep, and said, "Look after her! I'm going to find Aqua—she might do us some good for once!"

And maybe this would be our chance to make it up to the caravan for this afternoon, even if they didn't know there was anything to make up for.

The incident with the Dashing Hawkites that Darkness had attracted earlier had resulted in a number of injuries and damaged carriages.

At this point I was too scared to admit that the attack had been our fault and apologize, and I didn't like it. Maybe now I could do the right thing and soothe my conscience.

My eyes swept the area for any sign of Aqua.

"Eeeeek! What's going on?! Why did I wake up to find undead everywhere?! Kazuma! Dear Kazumaaaa!"

I looked toward the shout and saw Aqua, who had apparently been sleeping propped up against the carriage, faced with the rictus grins of the zombies.

Huh? Wait. No... No way.

"Stupid undead! How dare you try to attack me in my sleep! Lost souls, rest in peace! *Turn Undead*!"

At Aqua's shout, a gentle white light covered the area. Everyone who saw it let out an *ooh*.

As the light washed over the horde of zombies, they crumbled away one by one, purified...

And everyone who saw it went from *ooh*ing to cheering.

I, however, could only think one thing:

I'm so sorry.

"Ha-ha-ha-ha-ha-ha-ha! It was your mistake to show up when I was around! I'll send you all to your final resting places!"

Standing proudly in the light of the fire, she really was the image of a goddess sending lost souls to Heaven.

Watching her, I muttered quietly:

"...so, so sorry."

With Aqua hard at work, everyone else was already jubilant with victory. They heaped praise on my Arch-priest.

"What a beautiful priest...! Practically a goddess!"

"Look at her purify those zombies! She's with that Crusader who risked herself to save us this afternoon...!"

I'm sorry. I'm very, very sorry. I apologize for each and every one of my party members.

"Zombie attacks are pretty rare. Lucky for us that priest just happened to be along!"

Forgive me. If my goddess hadn't been here, you probably wouldn't have had this zombie problem.

"Easy as pie! How about that, Kazuma? Worthy of a goddess, wouldn't you say? I've worked pretty hard on this trip. An appropriate offering or two wouldn't go unappreciated."

I understood she naturally attracted undead, and I couldn't blame her for it. But when she sidled up to me looking so pleased with herself, I wanted to smack her.

"What?! Wiz, stay with me! Help! Wiz is—!"

I thought I heard Darkness calling frantically, but the leader of the caravan was already coming over to where Aqua and I were talking.

"You saved our necks again! Now I really will give you that reward, and I shall not take no for an answer!"

Deepest apologies, but you're going to have to.

Chapter 3

May We Sightsee in This Pathetic Town!

1

"Enjoy yourselves, then, and this wonderful hot-springs town! Really, you were such a tremendous help! Thank you so much!"

The caravan leader bowed repeatedly to us as he left.

Arcanletia: the so-called "city of water and hot springs."

This was where the long trip in that bone-rattling carriage had brought us.

I had actually tried to explain to the leader of the expedition that I thought this latest monster attack was probably our fault. But he just laughed at my "joke" and refused to take me seriously. He seemed convinced that I was just fabricating a reason why we couldn't accept any reward money. Frankly, that would be just as well for us.

But as we steadfastly refused any payment, he gave us several nights' worth of coupons for a hotel instead.

Apparently, he wasn't just a caravan leader but also the owner of the largest inn in Arcanletia.

He and the others were heading straight on to the next town.

"Ahh... Jarippa... I'll miss Jarippa...," Megumin muttered as she watched the carriage disappear into the distance.

Plenty of other travelers and adventurers had disembarked at the stop with us, but as they filtered away into town, Megumin stood and watched the departing carriage until it vanished from sight.

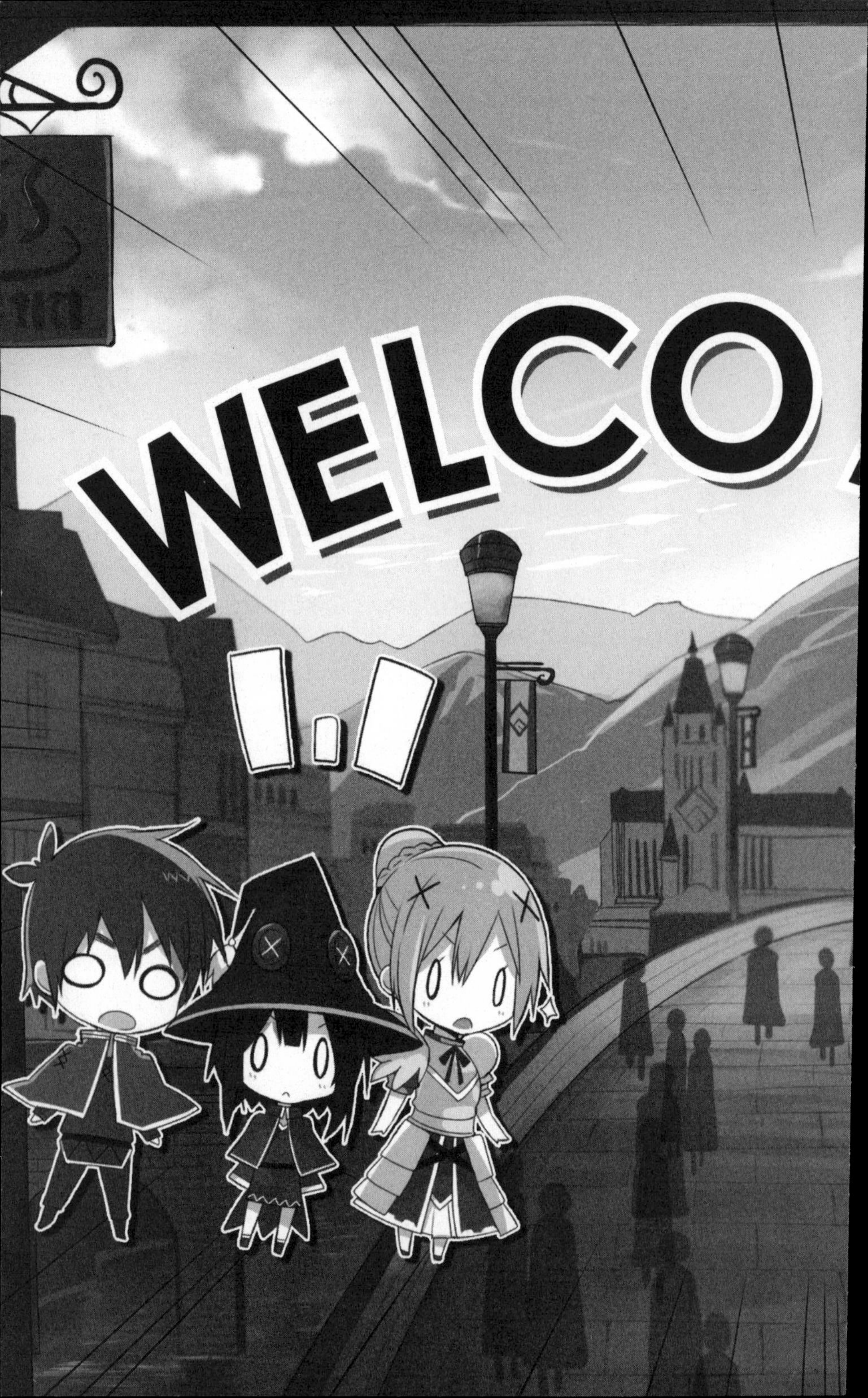
WELCO

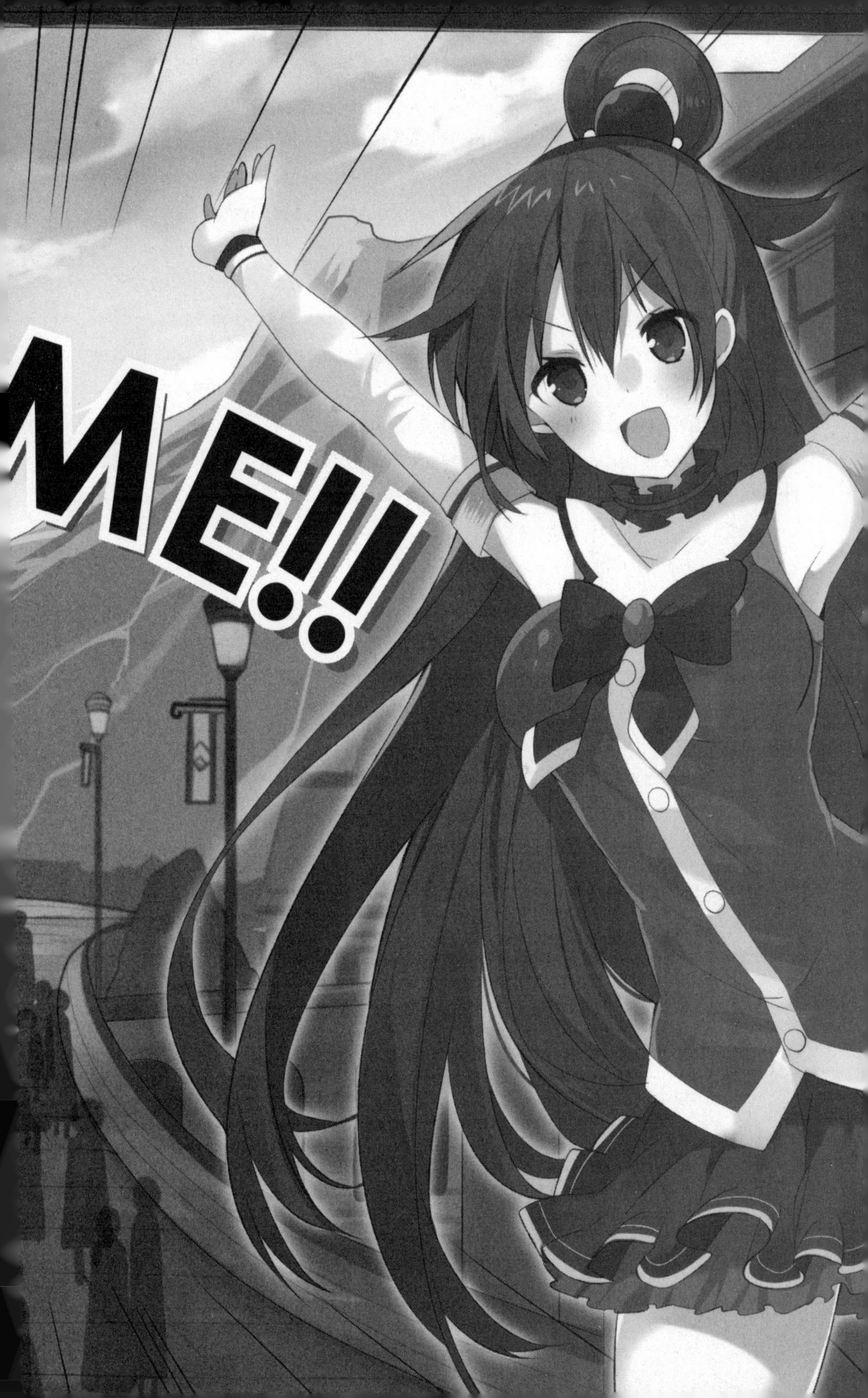
ME!!

"What in the world is Jarippa?" Aqua asked before suddenly realizing the answer. "Do you mean that baby dragon? Come to think of it, that rich-looking guy did say he wanted the 'great wizard' who had helped so much to name the thing."

…He asked a Crimson Magic Clan member to name something?

"I've heard that once named, dragons will never respond to another name as long as they live," Darkness said. I imagined that was pretty important.

Megumin nodded, appearing deeply moved.

"It seemed pleased with the name Jarippa. I placed a letter inside the cage for the owner, informing him of this name. I hope the owner will take good care of Jarippa."

What has she done?

After she had bestowed such a bizarre name upon my beloved sword, I could sympathize with the dragon's owner.

"You need to quit randomly doling out weird names to everything. It's time to admit to yourself that Crimson Magic Clan people can't name their way out of a paper bag."

"I admit *you* have no intuition for what makes a good name… Which is a shame, since you yourself have such a fine one. When you have a child, I shall name it for you."

"You're the last person I would ever ask to… Wait a second. Did you just say that 'Kazuma' somehow appeals to your Crimson Magic sensibilities? That's really depressing…"

I looked around town, carrying Wiz on my back. She was still unconscious after a certain someone's Turn Undead spell the night before.

And it was that very caster who now exclaimed:

"We made it! Arcanletia, city of water and hot springs!"

—Arcanletia, the aquatic, hot-springs capital.

Canals ran all around this town, which sat next to towering mountains home to natural geothermal springs and clear lakes. All the buildings were primarily blue, creating a beautiful skyline, and everyone seemed excited and happy.

It was striking to see such tranquility in a world afflicted by the Demon King's army.

Apparently, it had once seen battle with the agents of the King, but since that time, the enemy had diligently avoided it.

They claimed it was because the Demon King's army had found it difficult to fight a town with a large population of priests.

They claimed it was because this settlement was under the blessing of Lady Aqua, goddess of water.

They claimed.

"Welcome. It's so wonderful to have you here in Arcanletia. Are you here for sightseeing? Religious conversion? Adventuring? Baptism? If you've come seeking work, please, join the Axis sect! Right now, you can earn money simply by visiting other cities to expound the magnificence of the Axis Church! And it comes with perks: You get to call yourself an Axis disciple! Come on, now!"

Or maybe it was because there was a large population of Axis disciples in this city, and the Demon King didn't want anything to do with them.

We had barely arrived when a group of apparent Axis faithful approached us.

"What beautiful blue hair! Is that your natural color? I'm so jealous! I could die of envy! And that feather mantle looks like you got it from Lady Aqua herself!"

I looked over to where our resident deity was receiving a very enthusiastic welcome from a female believer.

...I think we could be in trouble here.

If she made with her "Actually, I *am* a goddess!" shtick, they'd be sure to call her an imposter and turn her into a punching bag.

People were already crowding around Megumin and Darkness, too.

Wiz was still passed out on my back. Small blessings, I guess.

Aqua, busy drinking in the praise for her looks, was the only one who seemed wholly pleased with the situation.

I worked my way close to her and whispered in her ear, "Hey, ixnay on the goddess-of-water stuff here, all right? I guarantee it'll get us in trouble. And try not to use your name. Come up with a fake one."

"Obviously, Kazuma. I'm not an idiot. But come on! Let's get to town! This is Arcanletia, city of water and hot springs! As the goddess of water, I could hardly be more excited! And best of all, this is the home base of the Axis Church!"

"?!"

The Axis Church. The one that's supposed to be full of weirdos. This was their *home base*?!

This religious sect, incidentally, also happened to worship Aqua as a goddess.

…No wonder she wanted to come here.

I could hardly leave the fidgeting goddess on her own, though, so I bowed to the Axis acolyte who had greeted us and said, "I'm sorry, but we already have an Axis priest. We're only here as tourists. Maybe next time…"

I was just trying to get away, but the believer waved at us and said with a broad grin, "I see—that's fantastic! Well, my fellows in the faith, may you have a wonderful day!"

Megumin and Darkness looked as relieved as I felt to be away from the evangelist.

But then…

"Welcome to Arcanletia! Axis believers often testify to the great things that happened to them when they believed: They were cured of illness, won the lottery, mastered an art. What could be in store for you when *you* join us?"

…*Who ever heard of such a pushy religion?*

As I warily eyed the zealous Axis welcome party, trying to keep my distance, I sensed the church itself knew I was avoiding it.

"…A-anyway, let's find somewhere to stay. I feel bad about basically scamming that guy, but since he gave us those hotel vouchers, we might as well use them and be grateful for it."

However, Aqua only smiled.

"You all go stay at that inn if you like. As an Arch-priest of the Axis Church, I can go to church headquarters, and they'll fawn over me!"

I didn't like where this was going.

We needed Aqua to stay and take care of Wiz.

"…Kazuma. I have a vague sense that things may go wrong with Aqua, so I will follow her. Could you take our luggage to the inn, please?" Megumin asked, watching Aqua with a hint of concern as the self-proclaimed goddess drifted away.

I had to admit, leaving her to her own devices seemed like an invitation for trouble.

So we left Megumin in charge of watching after Aqua, and the rest of us headed for the inn.

2

"Welcome! We heard all about you from the owner. Please, make yourselves at home!"

We arrived at the place indicated on the coupons to find a warm greeting.

I still felt a little guilty, given that the caravan had come under attack because of us.

The ambience was as impressive as you'd expect from a business claiming to be the largest inn in town. Frankly, traveling nobility might stay in a place like this. Given that this was a hot-springs town, I'd been picturing Japanese-style inns, but this reminded me of a Western hotel.

Apparently, this hotel was home to a bath with some renown even locally.

Employees came out to meet us and took our bags to our rooms without even asking us.

Once we got Wiz settled in her room, I finally found myself without any heavy items or cargo. And I was eager to do some sightseeing at the first town I'd ever visited outside of Axel.

We left a message with the staff to let Wiz know when she woke up that we'd gone out. I was a little worried about her, but my sitting there and watching her sleep wouldn't make her recover any quicker.

I was told life at this hotel really started in the evening, when more people arrived.

"What do you want to do, Darkness? Since we're here, I'm going to kill time wandering around until dinner."

"Mm, then I'll accompany you. I don't know too many places beyond Axel."

She was dressed casually, and she gave me a smile.

Now that I didn't have to cart anything around, I decided to take a stroll with Darkness.

This was a tourist town, and boy, did the merchants here know how to hawk their wares. Were we in a marketplace or a battlefield?

As we poked around one store, someone suddenly called to us:

"Sir, madam, if you shop at a junk emporium like that, people will start to wonder if you can even tell good merchandise from bad! I have 'Arcan buns,' made by elves from all-natural ingredients. Why not come over here and have a look?"

I raised my head to see the owner of the voice...

It was a handsome, pale-skinned man with long ears and green hair.

Yup: an elf.

"Shut yer trap! You're just a highway robber, is what you are! 'Good merchandise'? Expensive merchandise is more like it! Mister, stay here and try my meat buns, a dwarven specialty! These juicy morsels'll keep ya full all day—how's that fer value?!"

That was the owner of the shop I was currently visiting, shouting first at the elf and then at me.

He barely came up to my chest, but he was wider around than I was and sported a wild beard.

In other words, he was one stereotypical dwarf.

"An elf…! And a dwarf…! Look, Kazuma! An elf and a dwarf! Just like in the stories from when I was little!"

"I know! Elves are just as handsome as they say! And this dwarf is so stout!"

Darkness was as excited as a little girl, and I found it infectious.

Although they were merchants and not warriors or the like, they were probably the first really "fantasy-like" people I'd met since I got here.

An elf, noble and handsome.

A dwarf, rough and tough and sporting an awesome beard.

The sight of the two shopkeepers was a little overwhelming.

True, I'd seen elves and dwarves at a distance before, but this was the first time I'd ever actually talked to them.

My head was swiveling back and forth between them, my eyes sparkling with sheer awe at this fantasy world of wonders. But they didn't seem to take it quite that way.

"Look at all the trouble you're causing my customer," the elf said. "He wants to come see my merchandise, but he's terrified by your intimidation tactics. Let him go, you nasty dwarf."

"What's that?! I'll tell ya why he's upset—he's tryna see what I've got, and you won't let 'im be! He's gonna buy from me, so why don't ya shut that pretty face of yers and leave 'im in peace?"

With a fight brewing, I started to panic.

Come to think of it, all those old stories also mentioned that elves and dwarves didn't get along very well.

"P-please, both of you, don't fight. I-I'll buy! I'll buy from both your stores, so calm down!"

The dispute ended instantly, and the two shopkeepers smiled and chorused:

""Pleasure doing business with you!""

"Did you see that, Kazuma?! Elves and dwarves really don't get along! Just like in the stories my father used to read to me!"

We left the souvenir shops behind, Darkness still bubbling with excitement.

I ended up having to buy from both of them, but call it the price of a really interesting experience.

I couldn't shake the sense that I hadn't had much of a choice making my purchases, but Darkness seemed happy enough to cart the mountain of buns around on her back. She planned to share them with her dad and the servants when she got home. This being her first real trip out of town, she was eager to bring something back for them.

"They sure did fit your typical idea of elves and dwarves... Aww, man. I should've asked them about the best sights to see in town while we were buying these."

We were wandering around aimlessly, since neither of us knew anything about Arcanletia.

I told Darkness to wait a moment and went back to the shops. But neither shopkeeper was anywhere to be seen. Had they gone on break or something?

I peeked into one store and thought I heard a voice from inside.

Definitely. It was the elf from earlier.

...Wait a second. Is that the dwarf's voice, too?

No way...

"Hey, I thought you said you'd stop fighti—!"

Assuming they were continuing their argument from earlier, I leaped into the store...

"Oh, hey, mister. I wish you wouldn't come barging into our break room," the elf said, with none of the elaborate politeness of before.

...Wait. The elf... The elf...?

The elf (?) shopkeeper seemed to notice where I was focused. He gave a self-conscious tug on his ears.

"Oh, these? I know what you're thinking, but believe me, I'm a real elf, okay? Definitely not a fake one."

His ears... They were round.

They were basically as human as mine.

He was sitting there next to the dwarf with a pair of stick-on ears resting on his knees.

…And the dwarf was rubbing his very beardless chin.

"What… What's going on here?"

The elf (?) and the dwarf (?) exchanged a glance at my perplexed question.

"Well, you know. Forest elves have long ears because they stay away from humans. Elves like me, the ones who live in the human world? I mean, bloodlines mingle, and eventually you wind up with round ears. But then you try to tell customers you're an elf, and no one believes you. Or they're disappointed because you don't look the way they imagined. So I decided to try to live up to the hype," the elf explained.

…*What the heck?* You better believe I was disappointed.

The dwarf could tell, because he spoke up, too. "For me, there's a question of sanitation. I run that souvenir shop until sundown, but nights and mornings I'm a cook for guests at one of the inns. And I can't have a beard getting in all the food I'm trying to make, can I? …My, did you think we were still arguing? I'm sorry. That fight is just a little act we like to put on. I mean, everyone thinks elves and dwarves share such bad blood, right? We just ran with it."

It was like realizing that people at African tourist traps only held their spears when the tourists came around, then put them down and went back to their cell phones as soon as the gawkers were gone.

I guess it was dumb of me to be so eager to find fantasy elements in this world.

Both of them assumed apologetic expressions at my obvious disappointment.

"Aww, I'm sorry," the elf said. "Did I crush your dreams?"

"I suppose it goes to show you shouldn't assume, sir. There are dwarves with butterfingers in this world, just like there are elves who can't use a bow."

"Yeah—like us!"

The two of them burst into laughter.

...I really, really hate this world.

But let broken dreams lie. There was a reason I'd come here.

"Forget it. Don't worry, I won't try to return the merchandise. I just want to know if you guys can recommend any good sightseeing spots around town."

The two of them looked at each other.

"Sightseeing spots... Let's see, until a little while ago there was a hot spring I would have gladly recommended..."

"Oh yeah. If you'd come here just a bit sooner..."

"...? Aren't they all over the place? This is supposed to be a hot-springs town."

The elf gave a wag of his finger.

"Ah, but this was a mixed bathing spot favored by young women."

"You're kidding."

I took a step closer without realizing it.

The dwarf answered, "Oh yeah. We used to love going there when work was over."

Sounds like an amazing place. I wonder why you can't go there anymore.

The elf, reading my expression, said, "Truth is, a lot of the hot springs around here just aren't as good as they used to be."

"...A drop-off in water quality?

"Yep. Some of the people who used the baths got rashes or took ill. In the worst cases, they even lost consciousness. A specialist in hot-springs quality came in but never was able to figure out what was wrong."

I looked at the dwarf, who was wrinkling his brow.

Why did I have the feeling I was about to get dragged into something unpleasant again?

"—How'd it go? Is there anywhere good to see?"

Darkness's question reminded me what I'd actually gone back for. All the talk of mixed bathing had pushed it clear out of my head.

"Uh… How about we start by just wandering over that way?" I suggested to a very puzzled Darkness.

3

As the two of us wandered, I took in the sights, holding a skewer that I'd gotten from a food stall.

Canals crisscrossed the city, lending it an air of natural purity. Seemed like a nice place to live.

…Then, a young woman stumbling along under a heavy-looking load appeared ahead of us.

Darkness and I had moved to the side of the road, trying to make room for her, when…

"Oh no! What am I going to do? I just bought these apples—!"

Just as I was passing her, the girl lost her balance, and the contents of one of her shopping bags spilled onto the ground.

The woman scrambled to pick up the fruits as they rolled away. Darkness and I knelt to help her.

"Thank you so much! You're a big help. I wish there was some way I could repay you…!"

She nonchalantly dropped the shopping bags she'd been carrying so carefully, taking my arm.

Oh man. This was a flag if I ever saw one.

I didn't have a great feeling about the situation, but I had to admit I was curious where this would lead.

"The Axis Church runs a café just nearby," the girl said. "Let's go there and have a chat."

"…No thanks."

Darkness and I promptly turned to leave, but the girl grabbed us by the scruffs of our necks.

"Oh, don't be in such a hurry. I'm a fortune-teller, you know. Why not let me thank you by telling your future?"

"N-no thanks… We're all set, really… So let…go…!"

I managed to bat her hand away from my collar and made to run, but she grabbed on to my waist instead.

"I just figured out your fortune! If you go on like this, you will have very, very bad luck! But if you join the Axis Church, you can avoid it! So join now! Why not?"

"My bad luck was meeting you! Lemme go! Darkness, help me!"

Darkness gently grabbed the woman attached to my waist.

She took a small charm from her neckline and showed it to the woman. It must have been a symbol that identified her as a follower of Eris. Sort of the way the Cross identifies Christians on Earth, I guess.

"I'm sorry, but I already follow Our Lady Eris. If you want this man, you'll have to take him from me."

"Ptoo!" The woman spat on the street. Then she wordlessly released me, picked up her bags, and rushed off.

She looked back over her shoulder, apparently unaccustomed to such treatment.

"...Ptoo." She spat again and resumed making her exit.

Hang on...

"H-hey, Darkness. If... If the Axis and Eris Churches get that upset about each other, you ought to put that charm away... I mean, it's not a big deal, but...," I said, trying to be gentle with Darkness, who was still standing stiffly.

"...Hrk...!"

She grunted quietly and trembled.

......

"...You're kind of getting off on this."

"...Am not."

As Darkness and I walked along the relatively empty streets, suddenly a tough-looking guy and a cute young woman came running our way.

"Ahhhhh! Help me! You two there, please help me! That awful man tried to drag me into a dark alley! He probably worships Eris...!"

"Hah! Hey, mister! You're no Axis follower, are you? Heh! If you'd been some big, bad disciple of the water goddess, I might've run away. But since you're not, I think I'll be just fine! I have the blessing of the Dark Goddess Eris herself, so just stay out of my way—or you'll regret it!"

"Oh! How awful! And I have these Axis Church sign-up papers right here! If only *someone* would sign their name, they could scare away this dreadful disciple of Eris!"

....

I decided to pretend I hadn't seen anything and began striding away quickly.

"Oh, sir, please don't abandon me! Don't worry, if you just sign this paper, Lady Aqua will give you amazing powers of...something, and you'll be super cool! This Eris follower will no doubt flee in terror!"

"I sure will! Plus, if you join up, there are all sorts of mysterious perks. Some people get better at party tricks, and others suddenly find themselves very popular with the undead!"

Darkness pulled out her charm again and showed it to them.

"As you can see, I am an actual Eris follower. I'll thank you not to refer to her as the Dark Goddess in my—"

""**Ptoo!**""

Before Darkness could finish, the man and the woman both spat in the street and sped off.

...*Are* all *Axis people like this?*

Darkness stood wordless and stiff for a moment and then trembled.

......I could only assume she wasn't representative of most Eris worshippers.

And so it went.

"Congratulations! You are the one millionth person to walk down this street! Take this commemorative doodad—sponsored by the Axis Church! You only need to sign your name here, right where it says 'new believer.'"

I grabbed Darkness and did a one-eighty before we stepped down that particular avenue.

"...Huh? Is that you? Wow, I haven't seen you in forever! It's me! How have you been? Come on, you remember me! From school? We were in the same class? I guess maybe you wouldn't recognize me—I've changed so much since I joined the Axis Church!"

For starters, I didn't go to school in this world. And at the school I did go to, I certainly never had any female friends close enough to talk to me like that. So I walked silently past the girl on the street.

"...What's with this town? For that matter, what's with the Axis Church?"

Darkness and I had finally lost our Axis hangers-on and, thoroughly tired, were relaxing at an open-air café.

Darkness, sitting across from me, had encountered more than a little trouble thanks to the symbol of Eris hanging from her neck. Her cheeks were still red.

The waitress brought our orders as I collapsed over the table.

Plates arrived at our seat, accompanied by drinks.

I sat up, ready to eat...

"Oh, for our honored Eris-following customer. The owner sends this, with his regards."

So saying, the waitress set something at Darkness's feet with a metallic *clink*.

...It was a bowl of dog food.

"Enjoy your meal!"

The waitress smiled and bowed.

Darkness was red and quivering.

"...Kazuma. How about we all live in this town together?"

"...Absolutely not."

I stood up, done with my meal, and dragged the blushing, wet-eyed Darkness back to our hotel.

This place was weird in a number of ways.

...Speaking of which, as we were heading home, a girl, maybe about ten years old, came trotting up to us.

Then suddenly, she tripped and fell.

Darkness and I rushed over to her, whereupon she said painfully, "Oh... Thank you so much, miss and sir."

Then she smiled. I felt my bitter, cynical heart starting to heal.

"Are you all right?" I asked. "You should be more careful. Here, can you stand?"

I held out my hand to the girl, who took it happily. That guileless, innocent smile was doing my soul some serious good.

"Yes, I'm fine now! Thank you! ...You're so nice, mister. Could you tell me your name?"

"It's Kazuma. Kazuma Satou. And this scary-looking lady is Darkness."

Darkness gave me a gentle smack on the side of the head.

At that, the girl took out a pen and a sheet of paper.

"Kazuma Satou? How do you spell that? Could you write it down for me?"

"Sure, it's spelled..."

I took the piece of paper, only to notice the words written at the top:

AXIS CHURCH SIGN-UP SHEET

"Damn it all to hellllll!"

"Mister! Misterrrr!"

I ripped the paper clean in two.

4

The Axis Church.

With the exception of this town, this extremely minor sect was overshadowed by the Eris faith, which essentially served as the state religion.

Despite its size, though, it was remarkably well-known. If bandits on the road were to attack you, you could just tell them you were a member of the Axis Church. Your assailants would almost certainly flee in sheer terror.

That was just how scared people were of these fanatics. Even the Demon King's army supposedly kept its distance.

And at that moment...

"Dammit! Who's in charge here?! I'm gonna give them a piece of my mind!"

I had just charged into the church that served as Axis headquarters.

"Goodness, what seems to be the matter? Are you here to be initiated? Baptized? Or was it me you wanted?"

Inside the church, there was just one woman, sweeping the floor.

There was no one else there.

"Y-you... I mean..."

"Oh, don't be embarrassed; I'm only kidding. So serious. What were you expecting from a woman you just met? Maybe you should get your head examined."

I resisted the urge to punch this Axis nutjob right in the face.

"So, what does bring you here? Our high priest, Father Zesta, and all the other evangelists are currently out playing arou... I mean, working hard to spread the name of Our Lady Aqua. If you're looking for somebody, perhaps you could come back later..."

"Wait, no way did you just say that. They do all that obnoxious stuff basically for fun?! ...Never mind. Did a girl with a bandage over her eye and an Arch-priest with light-blue hair come by here? They're my friends."

The woman kept sweeping.

"Oh, they're friends of yours? Both of them are inside."

Deeper within the church? What are they doing there?

The woman cocked her head.

"By the way, your other friend...the one those children are throwing stones at. Is she going to be all right?"

"Huh? Ahh! Hey, you dumb kids, what do you think you're doing?! Get out of here, go!"

Darkness was in the fetal position just outside the church door, surrounded by children who were hurling rocks at her. I hurried to chase them away.

"K-Kazuma, l-levels are high in this town... Even the little girls overpowered me...! I don't think I'm going to survive...!"

"Just stay off the streets, for all our sakes. And put that Eris charm away already."

"No."

With my stubborn Eris-following fellow in tow, I went back into the church.

The woman inside indicated with her eyes a small room deeper in.

It was a little space just off the main entrance.

Huh. A confessional, basically.

"One of your friends is in there. As all our priests are away right now, we asked your honored Arch-priest to handle the confession booth."

Having your confession heard by an actual goddess? What a deal.

"Kazuma, I'll go find Megumin. You take care of Aqua."

With that, Darkness made to head farther into the building.

But the moment she drew alongside the lady with the broom, the woman swept the pile of dirt at Darkness.

Darkness came to a halt, her feet covered in dust and her cheeks bright red.

"Oh, pardon me! I saw your symbol of Eris and mistook it for garbage. I'm so very sorry."

"Not...at...all...," Darkness replied in a tight voice, trembling as though she was trying to restrain herself. Then she disappeared into the next room.

The scene further convinced me that I didn't want anything to do with this particular believer, so I made a beeline for the confession booth.

I tried the door, but it was locked from the inside.

I knocked, but there was no answer.

What was she, asleep?

With no other option, I went in the other door, the one penitents would normally use. The moment I entered, I heard:

"Welcome, my lost sheep... Now, tell me your sins. Your goddess will hear them and will surely forgive you..."

It was Aqua, completely lost in her new role and the atmosphere of the little room.

Apparently, she had heard a number of confessions already and decided she liked the job.

There was a partition between us, so I couldn't see her face, but I was sure she was smiling.

"I'm not your sheep. It's me. You know—me! Hey, what the hell is going on in this town? It's giving me a headache. I can't even be a normal tourist because of these loons. They're your followers, so do something about them!"

Aqua was silent for a moment, then...

"I see. You cry 'It's me! Me!' because you are a swindler, conning sweet old grandparents by pretending to be a relative in need. I accept your admission of guilt. You should reflect deeply, as deeply as you can, upon your crimes. If you do so, the goddess Aqua, in her infinite compassion, will surely forgive you..."

"No, you idiot, when I say 'It's me,' I mean it's *me*! What are you going on about? You're enjoying this, aren't you? You *like* finally being able to act like a real priest."

At that, Aqua fell silent again. "Do you have any other confessions to make? If not, then step out of the booth and gaze to the future with hope..."

"Hey, drop the act and listen to me already. They worship you in this town, right? You say a few words to the right people, and all this trouble is over. Take some responsibility!"

Yet again, Aqua went quiet for a moment. "Nothing else to confess? Then I shall be here, waiting for the next of my lost sheep... Now, be on your way."

"What are you...? Are you telling me to get out...?"

"Yes, get out! If you're done confessing, make room for the next person!"

This airhead must have decided she liked all the gratitude people showered on her for hearing their confessions.

Why was she so damn impressionable?

....

I adjusted myself on the chair and, in a deeply penitent tone, said, "...Actually, honored priest, there is something I want to get off my chest here."

"?! Tell me, tell me! Now, confess your sins; unburden yourself. Is it your profound interest in your Crusader friend's laundry? Your irresistible desire to bury your nose in the rich black hair of your spell-caster? The animal lust you feel for your beautiful, noble Arch-priest, despite your being an inept *hikikomori*?"

She sounded so pleased with herself.

I bluntly replied, "I broke the glass my friend the priest loved so much, the one she used to do party tricks. I stuck it back together with rice, sort of."

"?!"

"Oh, and once she was bragging about some terrific wine she had gotten, so I got curious whether it was really as good as she said. I was just going to have a little taste... But it was even better than I expected, and I accidentally drank all of it. So I just replaced it with cheap booze, since I figured she wouldn't be able to tell the difference."

"?! What are you talking about? Hey, Kazuma, what do you mean?!"

But I wasn't done confessing.

"And that priest... She just causes me nothing but trouble, so... before we came here, I posted a request for an Eris priest to join our party on the bulletin board at the Adventurers Guild."

"Waaaaah! You awful apostate, get ready for some divine retribution!"

Aqua tore open the little window between us with a clatter and tried to grab me.

"—Geez, calm down already. I told you, I was joking around. Anyway, Darkness and I couldn't even go sightseeing because of your crazy followers. Isn't this your home base? Try to keep a leash on them."

I was on Aqua's side of the confessional, having finally calmed her sobbing.

"What am I supposed to do about it? Today was the first day I ever met my own followers... And you aren't really looking for a new priest, are you?"

"First two things aside, no. No new priest."

"Hang on, what did you mean by 'first two things aside'?"

...Suddenly, a rap came on the confessional door.

No way someone had actually come to confess, right?

Not being a priest, I figured I probably wasn't supposed to be in here.

The door opened with a rattle, and someone shuffled in.

I poked Aqua next to me and indicated first myself and then the floor with my head.

Can I be here? was what I was trying to communicate, but Aqua assumed a grave expression, laced her fingers together in a praying gesture, and indicated a corner of the room with her eyes.

I followed her gaze to see a shadow on the wall and immediately recognized the crawling silhouette of Destroyer...!

Doesn't this idiot ever understand anything?

"Welcome, my lost sheep... Now, tell me your sins. Your goddess will hear them and will surely forgive you..."

No sooner had I made to leave the room than Aqua switched from triumphantly demonstrating her prowess at shadow figures to murmuring to her new penitent.

Just a second...!

"Yes... Please! Please listen! I am an Axis disciple who has long venerated Our Lady Aqua! But...! The statues of Eris... Her vast bosom...! It leads me astray! That bust is the bust of the devil! Please... Please forgive the grave sin of being tempted toward another goddess...!"

Dang. I wanted to go over and thwack this guy for coming to confess the stupidest possible thing.

But Aqua, with a completely straight face and not a hint of ridicule, said gently, "Be at peace, for you are forgiven. Love voluptuous and meager chests alike. In the Axis Church, all is permitted. Be it homosexual love, or the love of a person for an animal-girl, or a loli girl, or a NEET... As long as it is not an undead or a demon, and so long as no crime is committed, all is acceptable."

I noticed Aqua glance in my direction when she got to "or a NEET."

"Oh! Ohhh!"

The penitent seemed to be having paroxysms of gratitude. From the quality of his voice, I'd guess he was crying.

"O my pious believer. Let me teach you a holy invocation so that you will not be led astray by a devil. 'Eris's chest is padded.' Repeat these words any time you are tempted. And if you know any others facing this same temptation, you may teach them this mantra."

"'Eris's chest is padded'... I—I feel as though my eyes have been opened! Thank you for this wonderful invocation! You have my gratitude!"

And still gushing his thanks, the erstwhile sinner went on his way.

"...Hey, Aqua. Are you really comfortable throwing your junior goddess under the bus like that?"

"What are you talking about? For deities, the number of believers and the quality of their faith is very important. It's directly related to our power. I may not have as many followers as Eris, but mine are super-duper faithful. I'll do anything I have to, to help them."

G-geez...

When we left the confessional, we found Darkness, accompanied by a very tired-looking Megumin.

"Kazuma... You came..."

"What in the world happened to you? You look terrible."

In response, Megumin only shook her head.

"This is a wicked place. Let us go home quickly—now! I don't want to stay here another moment."

"S-seriously, what happened?" I was keen to know, but Megumin made no effort to reply.

The number of sign-up sheets bulging in her pocket, though, gave me a good idea.

"Are you going home, Milady Arch-priest? Won't you try this church's famous hot bath first? It's the best one in town, the very well-spring of the Axis Church. It's quite restorative..."

The one female believer who had been holding down the fort here pulled us aside.

"Huh, that sounds like a good deal," Aqua said. "How about it, everyone? Want to join me?"

"I want to go back to the hotel as soon as possible. Go back and rest. And Chomusuke seems frightened here for some reason. Perhaps she dislikes churches?"

"I can't say what might happen to me when the rest of the Axis followers get back. I'll count myself satisfied for today."

Thus Megumin and Darkness excused themselves, and then they stared at me, as if to ask what I was going to do.

"Is it mixed bathing?"

"If you say such untoward things in this holy place, you risk a punishment from the gods," the woman informed me.

So with that, I decided to leave, too.

5

Back at the hotel, we found Wiz in much better shape, warm and relaxed.

"Oh, welcome back, everybody! I'm sorry to have worried you. I went ahead and took a bath. I tried the mixed bath, on the advice of the staff. It's huge! There was no one there; I had it all to myself."

...*The mixed bath is huge?*

.........*Wait. She's feeling all warmed up... She went ahead and took a bath...*

So when I was in that stupid confession booth with Aqua, I could have been...

Psst.
The next two pages reflect the original
Japanese orientation, so read backward!

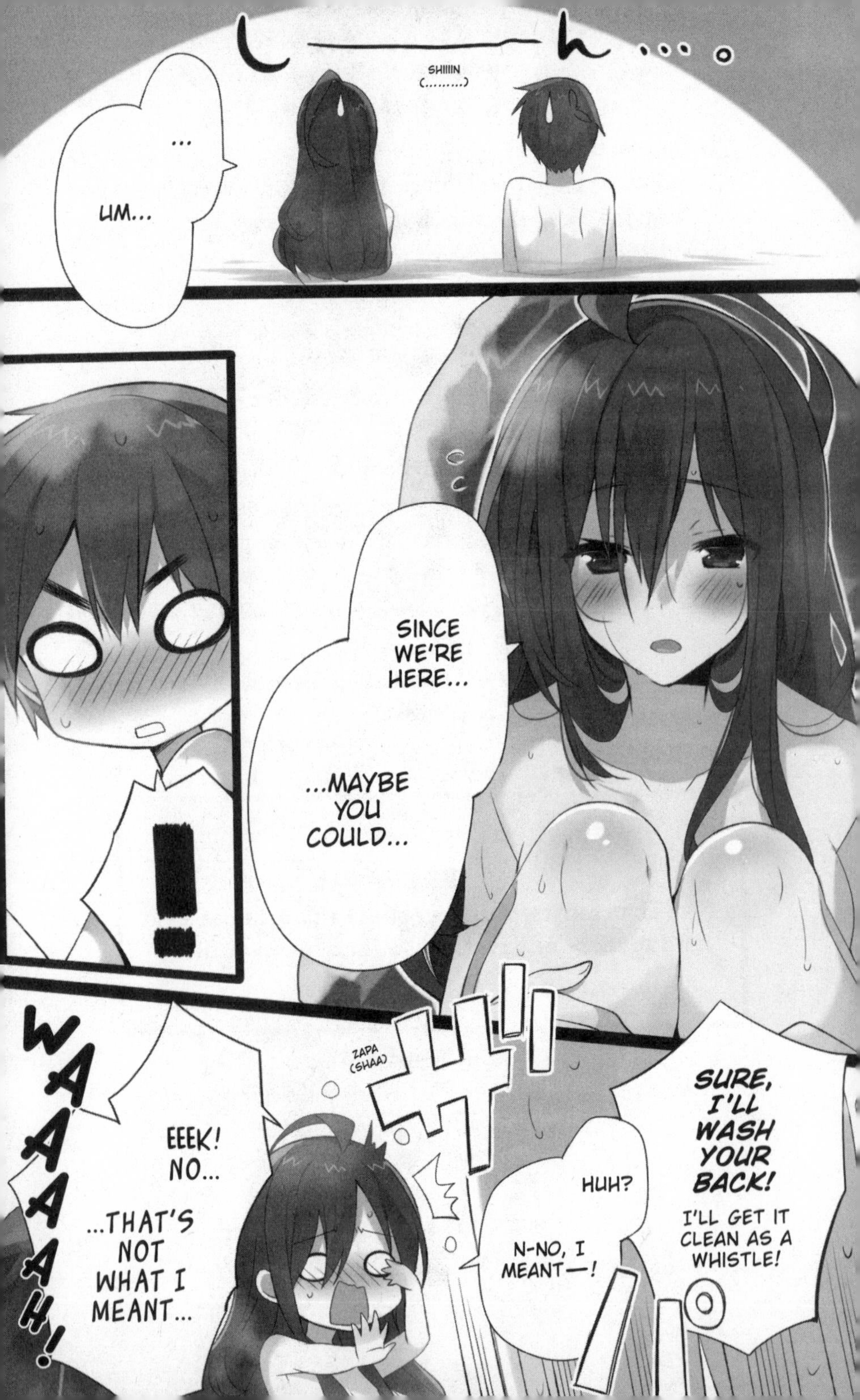
し———ん…。
SHIIIIN
(.........)
...
UM...
SINCE WE'RE HERE...
...MAYBE YOU COULD...
!!
SURE, I'LL WASH YOUR BACK!
I'LL GET IT CLEAN AS A WHISTLE!
HUH?
N-NO, I MEANT—!
ZAPA
(SHAA)
EEEK! NO...
...THAT'S NOT WHAT I MEANT...
WAAAAAH!

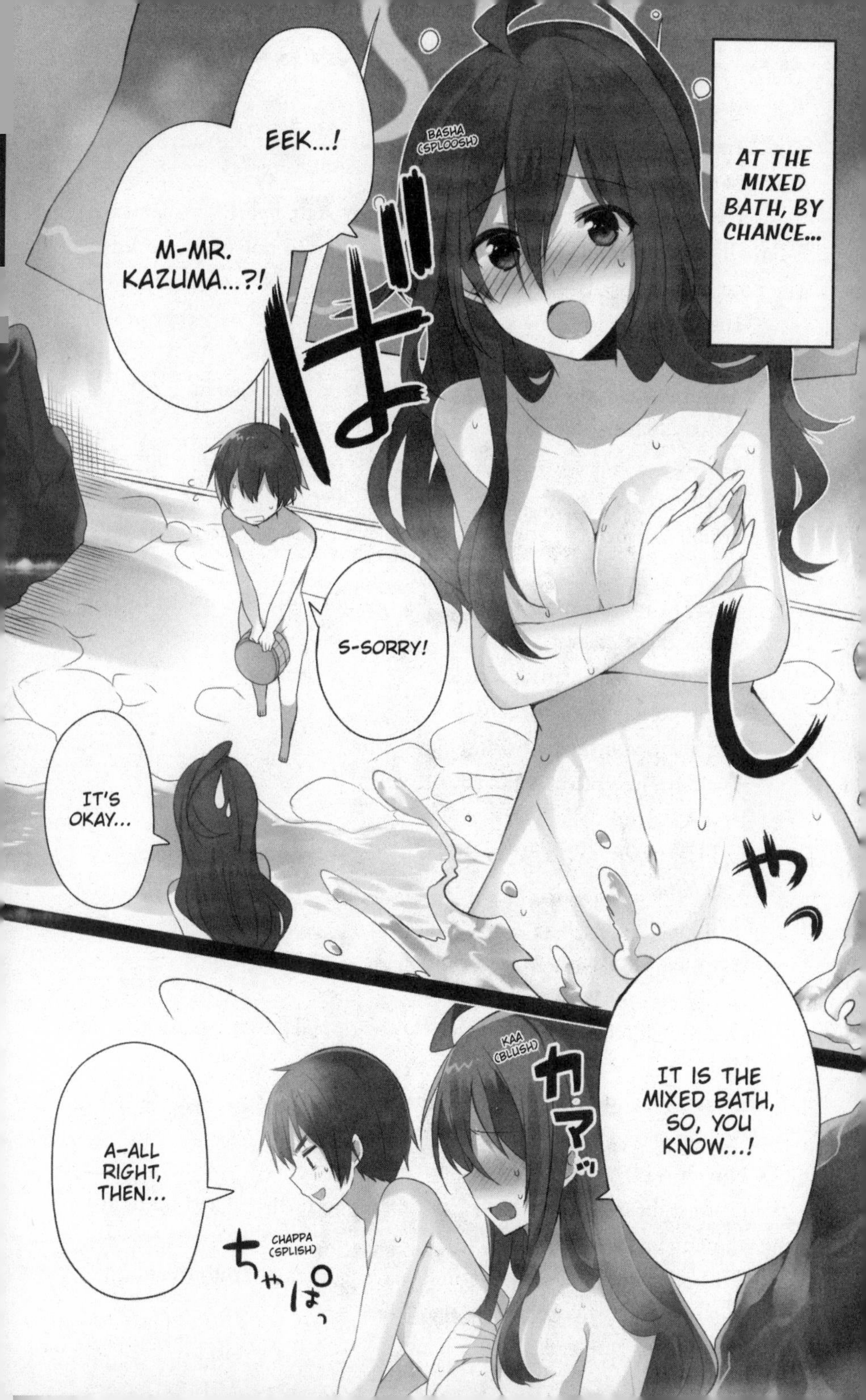
AT THE MIXED BATH, BY CHANCE...
BASHA (SPLOOSH)
EEK...!
M-MR. KAZUMA...?!
S-SORRY!
IT'S OKAY...
KAA (BLUSH)
IT IS THE MIXED BATH, SO, YOU KNOW...!
A-ALL RIGHT, THEN...
CHAPPA (SPLISH)

"And how was your sightseeing? Did you manage to see any...? Mr. Kazuma? Are you all right?"

"Y-y-y-yikes! Ten more minutes... Or at least five...! I—I mean, I-I'm all right! A-anyway, we didn't see squat. And I don't want to leave the hotel tomorrow. This town is weird."

"Those Axis followers are scary. Now I understand why they are as feared as the Crimson Magic Clan."

As Megumin and I explained wearily, Darkness broke in.

"M-maybe I'll go sightseeing again tomorrow..."

"Y-you're... You know what, do whatever you want. I'm gonna go take a bath."

I stood, exasperated at our Crusader, who appeared to be the only one who liked this town at all.

I went to my room to undress. As the only guy in a party full of women, I had gotten my own room.

But before I left, I turned back to everyone one more time.

"...I'm going to go take a bath."

"We heard you the first time. Have fun."

"I've been in already. Take your time!"

Thus Megumin and Wiz.

To Darkness, I said again:

"...a *bath*."

"Just go already."

Her tone couldn't have been colder.

Once I had returned to my room and stripped down, I made for the hotel bath.

I was a bit disappointed to go unaccompanied, but, well, that had always been a long shot.

Now it was time for today's main event.

From right to left there were the men's bath, the mixed bath, and the women's bath.

Without a moment's hesitation, I marched straight into the middle.

The changing room had a basket with clothes in it. In other words, someone was already here.

Okay, calm down. You don't know for certain that it's a beautiful young woman waiting in there.

I tried to steady myself as I stripped down, my heart beating just a little faster than usual. Then I went in.

I could hear someone talking in the bath.

"Now that awful sect is done for. Our plot to destroy their precious baths is done. Right now, everything is going to plan at the other places, too. If all goes well, we need only wait. We're long-lived—what's ten or twenty years to us?"

What was this, a manga or a movie or something?

Whatever it was, that man sure sounded like he was up to no good—

6

He'd just said, "That awful sect is done for."

I was sure he meant the Axis Church.

And then he had said, "We're long-lived—what's ten or twenty years to us?"

It was enough to conclude that someone who was not human was plotting to destroy the Axis Church.

…I am so, so sick of getting caught up in these dangerous situations.

And another thing. What would really be the harm if the Axis Church did get destroyed?

I hadn't been using Ambush, but luckily, the speaker didn't seem to notice me. I headed back toward the changing room, planning to ignore what I had just heard and get out of there before I got sucked in any further…

"Hans, you didn't have to come here just to inform me of that.

I keep telling you, I've come to recuperate in these very baths. Please don't involve me in your schemes."

I'd been halfway through re-dressing, but at the sound of a woman's voice, I immediately shucked everything off again.

"Aww, don't be like that, Wolbach. We could never get rid of this church with an open attack, and this is a chance to take them out. And I'll keep coming to make my reports, so you just keep bathing here in this hotel, all right?"

I wrapped a towel around my waist and strode up to the door, which I flung open with no warning.

""?!""

The noise clearly startled them both.

A man and a woman were in the bath. The man hadn't actually entered the water but was crouching on one knee next to the woman, with a towel wrapped around his hips. He was muscular and tall, with close-cropped brown hair, and was now watching me in surprise.

They must have been the ones making the evil plans.

But never mind that.

I was already fixated on the woman in the bath, who was eyeing me with a hint of nervousness.

She was a little older than me, with short red hair and unusual yellow irises reminiscent of a cat's. And she was generously endowed. Not bad at all.

As I stood there unable to tear my gaze away from the woman, the man started to whisper to her.

"Do you think he heard us...?"

"I don't know... But he won't stop looking at me..."

Their muted conversation brought me back to myself. I couldn't stare at the woman just because this was the mixed bath! I entered wearing the most nonchalant facade I could muster and then sauntered over to the washing area to clean myself.

I started dousing myself in water, feeling their gazes on me.

…Every once in a while, I couldn't keep myself from peeking back at the woman.

That was just the natural behavior of a healthy adolescent male, right?

"…Do you notice he only looks at me? What could it mean?"

"…Hrm, well…I suppose he didn't hear us. He doesn't look suspicious, just a little interested in you."

At that, the woman sank even deeper into the water.

Why'd he have to go and say that?

I finished washing and submerged myself in the bath a little ways away from the two of them.

I hadn't done anything to feel guilty about. No reason I should be circumspect around them just because I'd overheard them hatching some evil plans. And if I just happened to catch sight of the body of another bather, well, what fault was that of mine?

So I'd look, and I'd hold my head up high doing it.

"Hey. H-hey…"

"I-it's better than him being suspicious, isn't it? I've got stuff to do—see you!"

And he rushed out before he was finished speaking.

…It was only then that I noticed the man's body was completely dry. Couldn't he even enjoy a little soak while he was plotting destruction or whatever?

Or was there some reason he *couldn't* get in the bath?

…Anyway, I was there for my health. Who were these people, and what were they planning? I didn't know, and I didn't care.

Once the man called Hans was gone, the atmosphere in the bath took a turn for the awkward.

What should I do? I was getting nervous. Even I couldn't keep eyeing her when it was just the two of us.

I stretched in the water and let out a deep breath.

"...Ahem. You don't appear to be from around here. Are you on vacation?"

The woman suddenly spoke to me. Maybe she couldn't stand the strain in the air, either.

"I guess you could call it that. I just came to heal up in the baths with my friends."

She answered with an impressed "Oh," then continued. "What an interesting coincidence... I'm taking advantage of the curative effects of these waters myself. But you seem so young. What do you hope to heal in the baths? Are you hurt?"

"Yeah. I know I don't look it, but I'm an adventurer. We fought a powerful enemy recently, and I ended up taking a serious blow to the head. The stuff of legends, really."

She giggled at that and said, somewhat jokingly, "When I fought with my other half, I couldn't quite steal all my power back. So I'm here relaxing and trying to recover my original strength."

"Trying to get back your real power from your other half? There's a spell-caster in my party who would love to hear that."

"Heh-heh! Is she from the Crimson Magic Clan, by any chance? I wonder if the Crimson Magic girl I taught wizardry to is doing well for herself... If I could find my missing half, I wouldn't have to bother bathing to feel better. Maybe it's around here somewhere?"

She sighed deeply. I was pretty sure she was just poking fun, but her words somehow had a ring of truth.

"All right. I'm going to get out now... Oh, and...you might not want to spend too much time in the city's hot springs right about now."

I didn't quite understand what she was talking about, but she started to stand up...

"...Ahem... If you could...not stare too hard while I'm getting out of the bath... It's a most vulnerable moment..."

"Of course."

After my prompt answer, she seemed about to cry.

Well, nothing for it.

I turned my back and heard her murmur "Thank you." Then she muttered, "Ah… Here I finally find a nice hot-springs town. And now I have to find a new place to rejuvenate myself in the baths."

That sounded important. But she was already leaving.

Alone in the bath now, I thought back over what the pair had said. *"That awful sect is done for."*

And the girl had warned me, *"You might not want to spend too much time in the city's hot springs right about now."*

I had no idea why she'd said that, but I sensed she had done so with good intentions.

Did this mean they were plotting something for this town, the heart of the Axis Church?

Now that I knew about it, I was probably obligated to do something, but to be honest, it was hard to want to. I was so over getting sucked into crazy shenanigans.

…Right. I was here on vacation. I would just pretend I didn't know anything…

Just as I was busy ignoring reality, I heard it.

"Oh-ho! The bath at our mansion is nothing to sneeze at, but this is what you'd expect from a top-class hotel! You could practically swim in it!"

"Megumin, swimming in the bath is bad manners… Hey, what are you doing?! Why are you taking your towel…? Oh!"

"What are you so embarrassed about? It's just us girls. Are we not stalwart adventurers? Who are we to be so dainty and easily flustered?"

"That makes no sense! You're too mannish, Megumin! Oh, my towel—!"

I heard two very familiar voices from the women's bath.

Apparently, Megumin and Darkness had removed their towels.

I wanted to encourage them to keep it up, but I couldn't even see them—I would just have to use my imagination.

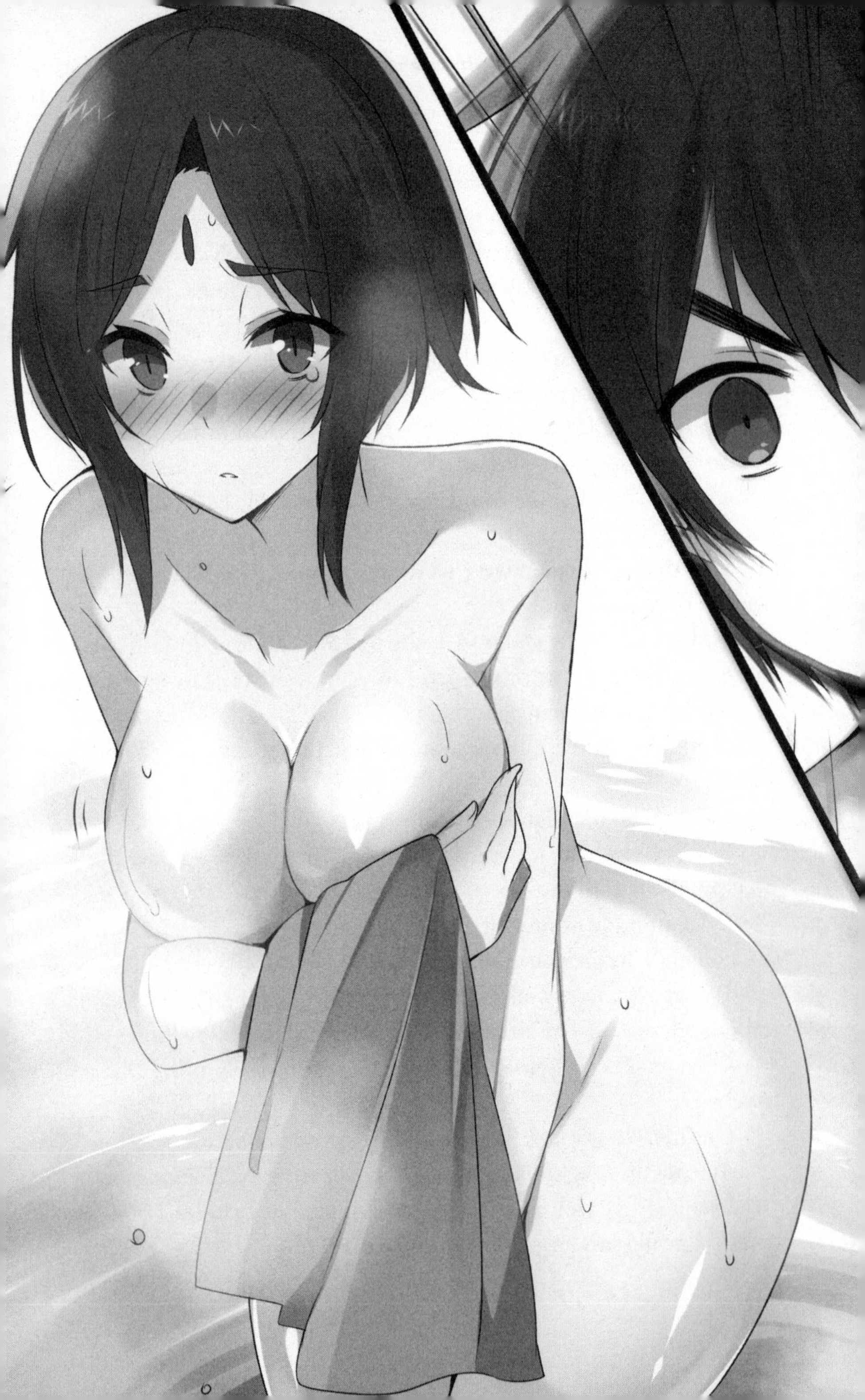

I casually waded over so I was closer to the women's bath. It was separated from the mixed bath by a wall that didn't quite reach the ceiling. If I piled up some washbasins and stood on my tiptoes on top of them, I might just be able to see over.

But I was far too much of a gentleman to do anything like that.

In comic books, that sort of thing ends with a shriek and a washbasin to the head, maybe a punch. But only in comic books.

This was reality, and trying to peek into the other bath would get the cops called on me, no question.

There came a *sploosh* of people getting into the water from just beyond the wall.

"Phew," said Megumin. "Having a soak in a hot spring once in a while isn't bad. Normally, I would not mind taking that stinky Kazuma outside and hunting the undead that Aqua always manages to find no matter where we go, but this was absolutely the right place for a getaway."

What did she just say…?!

"Is that why you recommended relaxing at the baths?" Darkness replied. "Well, I guess even if we'd stayed in town, we never would have gotten him to go out hunting. What is with that guy, anyway? Just when I'm sure he's a quivering coward, he shows a force of personality that would put most nobles to shame… He can't hold his ground against a Giant Toad, but he'll face down a general of the Demon King's army. He's so weird—or maybe he just doesn't make any sense."

"Shh! Darkness, hold on before you say anything else. The mixed bath is next door. If Kazuma had the choice between the men's bath and the mixed bath, which do you think he'd pick?"

"I see your point. He may be a timid screwup, but with an opportunity like this, he'd march right into the mixed bath."

Just wait till I get my hands on them.

Then again, nothing they had said was untrue. And I *was* in the mixed bath at that very moment.

Megumin and Darkness presumably had no idea of the conflict within me as they raised their voices.

"Kazumaaaa! We know you're in there! You've probably got your ear up against the wall right now, panting and trying to picture what part Darkness is going to wash first."

"M-Megumin! Why'd you have to make me the center of...! Hey, Kazuma, you're there, aren't you? I know you are!"

They could say whatever they wanted. I didn't have to let them know I was there.

It didn't even bother me that they'd read me like a book.

...Really, it didn't...

I stayed silent for a while, and finally, I heard whispers.

"That's strange. Could he not be there? Surely..."

"Hrm. But there's no answer at all..."

Still I didn't say a word. And then:

"It appears he really is not there. I suppose I misjudged him. I will treat him to some juice or something later."

"I guess it was a little rude of us. We shouldn't have judged him like that."

I could hear them quietly repenting of their accusations.

"Here we are bad-mouthing him, but he really is reliable. I'm sorry I was so suspicious of him..."

"Yeah. He may not look the part, but he really comes through when his friends are in trouble. He isn't always very open, but deep, deep down, he's a good guy. I'm sorry, too..."

I was getting a twinge of guilt about eavesdropping on them now.

Once I got out of the bath, maybe I would treat them to something instead.

I was just about to leave the bath when—

"By the way, Megumin, I keep wondering about that thing on your butt..."

"Oh no! I know we are friends, Darkness, but if you say another word, I will not let you off easily!"

"Hang on—! Stoppit—!"

There was a violent splashing, and bathwater came flying over the wall between them and me.

"Good heavens! Such outrageous behavior! If you have time to worry about my rear, how about you spend some of it making these distractingly huge things more compact?!"

"Ahh! Hey! M-Megumin, stop—! Those are my—!"

It didn't take long for my pangs of conscience to vanish and for me to reassume my position at the edge of the bath.

Then, just to be safe, I activated my Ambush skill and put my ear to the wall…!

"Now!"

"Hi-yah!"

"Bwah?!"

The sudden impact came straight through the wall and into my temple, sending me tumbling into the water. Darkness must have given the wall her best smack from the other side.

"Did you hear that?! I knew he was there!"

"Yeah! We had his number! That shameless ogling I feel from him every day! I knew someone with that much frustrated lust would wind up in the mixed bath!"

I heard their triumphant voices, my head throbbing from the blow.

Now I was definitely gonna kill them.

"*Create Water!*"

""Yeeeeek!""

I fired my magical spray upward, aiming for the opening at the top of the wall. On the other side, the girls shrieked as it poured down on their heads.

Sundry items came flying back from their side in a counterattack. Shampoo, soap, a wash bucket, Chomusuke.

"Hey! Don't fling your cat! She almost ended up in the water!"

"I keep meaning to wash her, but she hates baths. I end up covered in scratches every time I try. As your punishment for eavesdropping, you must do it," Megumin asserted.

Chomusuke was digging her claws into my arm in terror of the water.

I guess it's no walk in the park for you, either, having such a crazy owner...

Now that they knew I was here, there was no reason to hold back.

"Heeeey, since we finally got to go on a hot-springs vacation and all... Us party members are basically family, aren't we? Since we're here, come on over to this side and join me. Both of you have been in the bath with me before, so why not now?"

"This man usually treats us as nothing but trouble, but listen to him now—party members! Family!"

"I can't tell if you're a total screwup or the gutsiest person I ever met!"

—I chose to get out of the now-tempestuous bath and return to our room before they did. But...

"It—it's not faiiiir! I...! I didn't do anything wrong...! I only got in the bath!"

"It must have been awful, Lady Aqua... B-but please d-don't cry... Your tears burn terribly when they touch my skin..."

...I found Aqua weeping, her face buried in Wiz's chest.

"Geez, look at you. What crazy thing happened now? How many people do you plan to cause trouble for today?"

"What do you mean, crazy?! And what do you mean, trouble?! Why are you so sure *I* did something wrong?!" Aqua spat, whipping around.

"Apparently...Milady Aqua got in the most cherished bath of the Axis sect, one full of good minerals and everything, only to have it turn into regular hot water. So..."

"So they chased me out! Me, their goddess! How could I get run out of my own church?! How?!"

I recalled other occasions when Aqua had purified water with an accidental touch.

"And…!" she went on. "The manager of the bath was furious. And I said to him…! I said, 'I'm sorry for turning your hot spring into regular water. But it was only natural! Because I'm the water goddess Aqua herself!' And the manager…*sniff*…he just snorted at me! 'Pfft.' Even though it's true! I really *am* a goddess!"

Wiz offered comfort as best she could as the goddess burst back into tears.

I only stared at Aqua…

"…Pfft."

"Waaaaaaahhh!"

"Mr. Kazuma!"

1

You could get food on the first floor of our hotel.

"It looks like the dangers of this town are really risky," Aqua said as we ate our classy, healthy, and surprisingly delicious breakfast.

The dangers are really risky? What does that even mean? She should learn how to use words.

"You were up all last night crying. What are you on about now? The biggest danger to this town right now is your special power. Don't use any of the baths except the outdoor one attached to our room, okay?"

That caused Aqua to smack the table.

"Listen to me, will you?! I don't go around purifying hot springs just for fun! I dumped all of Darkness's expensive bubble soap in the bath at home as an experiment, and even then I cleansed it right away. So of course I would purify a hot spring."

"What?! You used all of it?! I brought it back special from the Capital!"

Aqua ignored Darkness's pained exclamation and continued.

"But it's weird. It took ages to purify the special bath at the Axis Church. And I have superstrong purifying powers. For example…"

Suddenly she stopped speaking and stuck her finger into the cup of coffee I was about to drink.

Instantaneously, the black coffee became clear hot water.

Everyone looked at Aqua. She cocked her head.

"...See?"

"'See'?! You dumbass, go get me a new cup of coffee!" I demanded, setting down my mug, but Aqua just licked the tip of her finger.

"That's how it usually goes. If it took that long to purify the bath, it must mean it was really polluted... And don't you think the quality of the hot springs around here has suddenly gotten worse? Maybe it means the Demon King, unable to defeat my Axis Church in open combat, is trying to steal away the precious wellspring of their faith!"

""Oh. Wow.""

"*Please* believe meeee!"

Darkness and Megumin offered a simultaneous non-answer, and Aqua pounded the table.

Her reaction practically caused question marks to appear over their heads.

"So some hot springs have gone bad," Darkness said. "What makes you so sure it's the work of the Demon King's army?"

"I know people try to keep their distance from the Axis Church and often find it generally disagreeable, but who would go to that kind of trouble?" Megumin said.

It does seem like an awful lot of work...

Dammit. I guess that meant the guy I'd seen in the bath yesterday really was an agent of the Demon King. He did say something about having messed with the bath in the Axis Church. I was glad that Aqua had accidentally thwarted that plan and all, but...

What should I do? Should I tell everyone?

But if I did, I was sure it would blow up into this huge thing. We would have to report it to the Adventurers Guild in this town, and we would have to spend our time helping out, too.

Our precious vacation would go down the drain, and we'd end up having to deal with yet another of these obnoxious Demon King types.

Call it intuition, but those two in the bath yesterday seemed really powerful.

I mean, they had marched right into the heart of the Axis faith to soak in the baths, and they were apparently planning to bring it all down with only the two of them.

As for me, just the other day I fell out of a tree and died trying to fight the weakest monsters in the area. I didn't think I was much of a match for them.

"I'm going to stand up and defend this town! You'll all help me, right?" Aqua said.

"Sorry," I answered, "I'm busy, uh, walking around town and stuff."

"I got quite enough firsthand experience of the fearsomeness of Axis disciples yesterday. I don't need any more today. I shall stick with Kazuma," Megumin said.

Neither of us had the slightest interest.

"What?! Why?! You can go for a walk anytime! And, Megumin, how can you hate my sweet little followers so much? D-Darkness, surely you…"

"Er…I'm, uh… You know…"

"Pleeeease!"

"Okay! I'll help you! I'll do it! Just get away from me before you purify my grape juice!"

Something occurred to me as I watched Darkness cave to the weeping, clinging Aqua.

"Hey, isn't Wiz up yet? She seems like a soft touch, especially with you. I'll bet she'd go along if you asked."

"I spent all night crying on her shoulder. By morning, my tears had made her pretty much transparent. So I think I'll let her rest for now."

"Help Wiz before you help the town! It's your fault she's done nothing but sleep since we got here!"

After Megumin and I watched Aqua drag Darkness away, we settled down to deciding what to do for the day.

For a resort destination, there was surprisingly little to see around here.

We could certainly just wander around, but that seemed it would invite the flood of "evangelists" again.

As I stood there thinking, Megumin gave a *let's go* tug on my sleeve.

"If we have no particular place to go, then please accompany me to set off an explosion outside town."

"We came all the way here, and *that's* what you want to do?"

Megumin's daily explosion was practically part of the scenery in Axel, but a sudden blast would probably disturb a tourist trap like this.

Oh well. If we got far enough away from town, it shouldn't be a problem.

So I told Megumin I would go with her for her explosion, and she sipped her juice happily.

"Good morning… Oh… You're all up so early…" Wiz appeared, groggy and pale and disheveled as she dragged herself into the room.

"Morning. You feeling better? I heard Aqua had you vanishing."

"Yes… For a moment there, I thought I saw one of my party members from my adventuring days waving to me from across a river… But I'm doing okay now."

Sounds like she really had it rough. Wasn't that what they called a near-death experience?

Come to think of it, can undead even have near-death experiences?

"Got anything in mind for today, Wiz? Megumin and I were planning a trip out of town."

"I didn't have any particular plans… So you're thinking of leaving? The monsters that live around here are pretty strong, you know. If it's all right, maybe I should come with you."

I was so grateful that she'd said that. And I hadn't even had to ask her.

"Absolutely! I'll feel so much safer with a real wizard along."

"Hey! Would you mind informing me as to where this fake wizard might be?!"

2

Before we headed out of town, we decided to amble around a bit, since we were here and all.

We had yet to encounter any overzealous Axis types.

Megumin walked ahead of us in high spirits, Chomusuke on her shoulder.

I watched her stride along as I asked Wiz beside me, "Hey, Wiz. Earlier, you mentioned a party member from your adventuring days. And it got me wondering... Why did you become a Lich? I know I'm not really one to talk, but I feel like you're one of the few halfway mature people in Axel. I'm just not sure what would drive a famous adventurer to go against the laws of nature and become a Lich."

I knew my question probably came out of nowhere, but I'd been wondering about this for a while.

I'd met another Lich beside Wiz: Khiel, in that dungeon. He had said he became a Lich when he had no other way to protect the person he loved.

Wiz thought for a moment, then said, "That's a good question... It's a long story, so maybe I could wait to tell it until Lady Aqua is with us, too?"

She smiled innocently.

Well, if that was what she wanted...

I had no idea what her story was, but it was possible that knowing it might soften Aqua's attitude toward her.

I agreed we could wait for the self-proclaimed goddess. Wiz smiled.

"Good. Maybe we could get Mr. Vanir to join us to talk about the old days. He and I had quite a battle once, when I was an adventurer."

Now that *I want to hear.*

And I'd certainly like to know how she went from an epic battle to friends with that guy. And now that I was thinking about it...

"Hey, what's with this 'old days' business? How old were you when you became a Lich?"

"I was twenty."

Huh.

"I see. I guess that is about how old you look. So how long has it been since then? I mean, how old are you now?"

"Twenty. I haven't aged since becoming a Lich."

"No, but I mean…"

"I'm always going to be twenty, no matter how many years pass."

"A-all right."

She didn't seem to want to pursue the subject, so I decided not to press her.

You weren't supposed to ask a woman's age, anyway.

Then suddenly Megumin spoke up from ahead of us. "I have been meaning to ask you, Wiz. Are there others in the Demon King's army beside you who can use Explosion? I mean…any other large-breasted young women?"

Well, that came out of left field.

"No, as far as I know, I was the only one in his army who could use explosion magic. But I haven't been to the castle for a very long time, so it's possible someone else came in after I left…"

"I see. That is good to know." Megumin breathed a sigh of relief.

Except that wasn't good at all.

"Hey, what do you mean 'large-breasted young women'? Don't just end the conversation like that. Explain it to me, too."

"You are such a… Well, it's nothing important. One of the reasons I came to Axel was because I had heard there was a female spell-caster there who could use Explosion. I guess that must have been Wiz."

"Hmm. And what do the big boobs have to do with it?"

"You could at least say 'a woman with big boobs' or 'a well-endowed spell-caster.' Anyway, she's the person I'm measuring myself by. I hope to meet her one day…"

"…Measuring yourself by? You mean, like, in terms of bust size?"

"I shall kill you now."

I shoved my hand against Megumin's forehead to keep her away as she threw herself at me, staff raised.

"Huh…? I could swear I just saw someone I knew…"

Wiz was looking toward the most hot-springs-dense part of town. I followed her gaze and saw…

"Okay, Megumin, Wiz! Let's zip on out of town, fire off our spells, and see some sights!"

The vision of *him* inspired me to hustle the two of them out of there.

The guy Wiz thought she recognized was the one having a suspicious conversation in the bath the day before.

Now I was sure: If Wiz knew him, he was unquestionably connected to the Demon King.

Please, stop already! I'm just a totally normal, totally weak adventurer with no powers or anything! Please, please don't let me get dragged into anything else dangerous!

"That is a good idea. We should go sightseeing once I have released all my pent-up explosive energy for today. Wiz will help us stay safe. Let us find a monster and explode it!"

"Oh, Mr. Kazuma, there's no need to rush! …Hmm, who *was* that, anyway?"

I couldn't let Wiz and that guy run into each other. I couldn't say quite why, but I was sure it would be trouble.

3

Maybe it was because of the abundance of pure water in this area, but as soon as we got out of Arcanletia, we found a vast forest.

"Let us go to that forest! I'll bet there are scads of monsters there! Let's hunt some of them! Come on, quick!"

Wiz and I followed after the unusually bloodthirsty Megumin.

I activated my Sense Foe skill, and what do you know? Sure enough, I detected plenty of monsters in there.

"Boy, the place really is crawling with them. Actually, it seems like they know we're here. I wonder why they don't attack us."

I could sense them, but I couldn't see them.

"They're probably cautious because we just came out of Arcanletia," Wiz said. "Most of the people who come from the city are Axis followers, so… I've heard even monsters keep their distance from them."

Axis disciples must be the loneliest people in the world.

"Or…it could be because I'm here. It's possible they avoid Liches instinctively." She gave a sad smile as she said that.

I do have a tendency to forget that Wiz is actually one of the generals of the Demon King's army, even if a rather lackadaisical one. She might not look like much, but you don't get a job like that for no reason.

I also recalled how when Beldia showed up, and then again with Vanir, the weaker monsters near town stayed hidden, keeping clear of our powerful visitors. It was entirely possible they were keeping their heads down, intimidated by Wiz's power.

I had been living in Axel for a while at this point, but I had never heard of any monsters actually invading the town. I wondered, a bit surprised, if it had something to do with Wiz living there.

"Hrm. Well, no choice, then. I will just find a spot over there somewhere to perform my explosion. I so wanted to take out some monsters, and perhaps raise my level to boot…"

After this obnoxious pronouncement, Megumin began intoning her magic.

She had a huge amount of magic power in that little body.

I still couldn't fathom how someone could be powerful enough to use a spell like that and then waste it in a field someplace. I honestly believed there was a variety of ways to use it that might have benefited society.

As I mulled over this, Megumin finished her preparations.

"*Explosion*!!"

She really had chosen a random place. A magical blast blossomed, shaking the air and rumbling against the earth.

Trees were uprooted, the ground heaved, and with a swath of destruction, Megumin left her mark on the forest.

The woods filled with noise as the sudden tremors sent every bird scrambling out of every tree.

"Phew! Shall we go back now? I will need a ride, of course."

The perpetrator of the massive blast was calmly lying facedown in the dirt.

She seemed so sure about that piggyback ride. For a moment, I considered leaving her there.

"You need a ride every time. Can't you use your magic a little more efficiently? Here, I'll give you some of my MP, so get up and walk."

I used Drain Touch to transfer some of my magic. Maybe I didn't transfer enough, because Megumin still wobbled noticeably when she stood.

Then she checked her Adventurer's Card, and a smile came over her face.

"Ooh, it seems I caught several unsuspecting kobolds in that blast. They're listed in the space for monsters I defeated today."

...*Uh-oh.*

Weren't we just talking about how my level was the lowest of all of ours right now? And it still was, even though I had gained two levels after our battles with the Lizard Runners and the Dashing Hawkites. *Maybe I should use the skill points from those levels to get a decent attacking skill that might help me level up even more.*

I was still ruminating on the possibilities when:

"...Hmm? Something's coming this way. And fast, to judge by Sense Foe."

"Oh? Perhaps it was drawn by the sound of my explosion."

Whatever it was, it was approaching from the depths of the forest. Even with my Second Sight skill, I could see only a dark shape.

Wait...

I knew that shape.

This was a monster that coexisted with weaker creatures like goblins or kobolds. It basically looked like a saber-toothed tiger covered in black fur.

"Haaaarrrrr!"

It was the natural enemy of the novice adventurer: the Beginner's Bane.

"Wiz! Wiz! You gotta do something!"

"Snipe it, Kazuma, snipe it!" Megumin cried. "There is still enough distance—you can stop it!"

"I left my bow with the rest of my equipment back at the hotel!"

"If I ever said you were reliable, I take it back! If that is your attitude, you will be lucky to be half my level!"

"Moron! Who got that thing's attention in the first place?! Maybe I oughta just Drain my magic right back and leave you here!"

"Calm down, both of you! I'll handle this somehow. You both just keep back." Wiz stepped forward as if to protect us both.

I decided to do what little I could, using Create Earth to make some sand I could throw in the creature's face.

Megumin stood close behind me.

Wiz showed no sign of using magic, despite the onrushing Beginner's Bane.

"Hey—hey, Wiz? Wiz?"

"Oh no!"

Before our eyes, the Beginner's Bane jumped on Wiz.

The monster was as big as a cow; it easily pinned her to the ground.

As Megumin shouted behind me, I raised my hand and prepared to use wind magic to blow dust into the thing's eyes...

""Huh...?""

The enemy on top of Wiz was suddenly sound asleep.

She crawled out from under it. I would have expected her to at least be scratched up from when the monster first attacked her, but there was no sign of injury.

"Now I remember," Megumin said. "Liches only take physical damage from magical weapons. And they have the ability to inflict a variety of status conditions on their opponents beyond their basic ability to drain HP and MP. Poison, paralysis, sleep, and curse. Wiz didn't even need magic to deal with this enemy."

Wow. Liches are really something.

Aqua might be able to make her translucent, and Vanir might be able to fry her—but those things seemed so irrelevant now.

"Phew... Well, shall we head back?" Wiz brushed the dust off her clothes and smiled.

4

When we got back to town, there was a huge crowd right in the middle of the leisure district.

"What's going on? Is there an event or something?"

"I wonder. Given this is a tourist town, perhaps they have some performers or something to entertain visitors."

Megumin and I, our interest piqued, made our way over.

"...Oh, that's Lady Aqua. What's she doing there?"

Aqua stood smack in the middle of the crowd.

What was she up to? She stood on a wooden box, holding something that looked like a megaphone. Next to her, Darkness was bright red and trembling from embarrassment.

I recognized the object in Aqua's hand as an item enchanted with wind magic, but what was she doing with it?

As if to answer my question, Aqua began shouting.

"My beloved Axis followers! The Demon King is working to destroy this city even as we speak!"

Darkness hung her head in embarrassment.

"How, you ask? He has poisoned the city's hot springs! I have confirmed that many baths have already been affected!"

Had she spent the entire morning just going to hot springs?

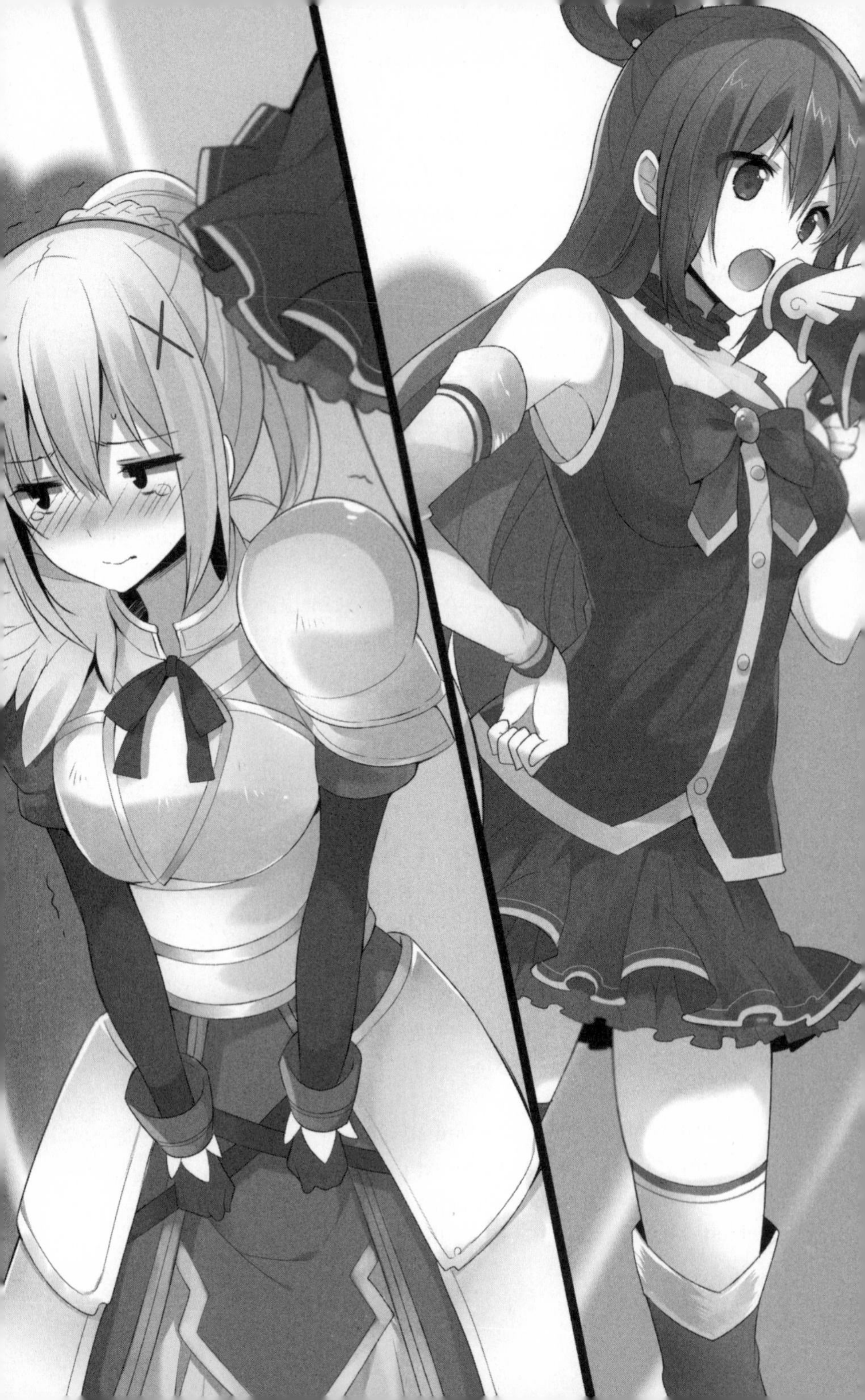

"What are you talking about? I was just in one of the hot springs, and I'm fine," an onlooker said.

Aqua nodded assiduously and replied, "That's because I've been around to each one and purified it. All the baths in this area are safe. But this isn't over yet! That's why I have a request for all of you. Please do not go in the baths until this incident is resolved!"

That set the crowd muttering.

Aqua poked Darkness, standing next to her.

On the verge of tears, the Crusader twitched as if she was about to say something, but then she kept quiet.

An old guy pulling his vendor's cart along commented, "Miss Priest, this is a hot-springs town. And it'll be a ghost town if you tell everyone not to go in the baths."

"He's right. Why would the Demon King poison our bathwater, anyway?"

The people began whispering among themselves.

"It's—! Because he wants to get rid of this city's tourism industry, so the Axis Church won't get any more money! That's right! The Demon King is afraid of you Axis believers! I promise this is not just something I'm making up because I'm bitter about being the only one who can't go in the baths! Now, honorable Axis followers—!"

Then...

"There you are! Hey, you! What did you do to the hot spring at my hotel?! It's turned into regular hot water!"

From beyond the crowd, a man stood glaring at Aqua. Probably the owner of one of the hot springs. Along with him were several other guys with alarming expressions.

"You were right—she is here! Grab her, everyone! She's been playing an awful trick at all the hot springs—she turns them into plain water!"

"Yeah, maybe *she's* the one the Demon King sent to try to destroy our town!"

Sigh.

How did she expect to help the city if she went around sabotaging all the hot springs?

"N-n-no, I'm not! There's a reason for this! Please, listen to me! Those baths I purified, there was poison in them! I admit, I might've gotten rid of the special minerals along with the poison—but it was all to help you…!"

"If that's true, you could have at least said something to us! Anyway, there's no way you could purify so many baths! Word is, you waited until there was no one there before you got in the hot springs. Then you snuck in and changed our bathwater for regular water!"

"N-n-n-no, I didn't! If anyone had seen me doing my purification, they might have realized who I really am! And then there'd be an awful commotion—!"

This was not good. She was going to say something she shouldn't at this rate.

"Hey, Megumin, Wiz! Let's get out of here before those two notice us! Just pretend we have nothing to do with this!"

"What?! Are you simply going to let this continue? I think you are the only one with any chance of helping—say something to them!"

"Lady Aqua looks ready to cry! Mr. Kazuma, if this keeps up—!"

As they spoke, I looked over at Aqua.

One of the hotel owners began shouting. "I'd say there's already a commotion! And it's already awful! So who *are* you, really? Maybe an agent of the Demon King?!"

"Huh?! N-no! Come on, Darkness, don't just sit there—say something! Just like we discussed! You say, 'O Axis Church! Axis Church, please help us!' Don't be shy—say it!"

"A-Axis Church, p-please…," she whispered, red-faced in front of the massive crowd of onlookers.

I couldn't help but feel sorry for her.

"Argh, fine! I'll reveal my true identity here and now, then! O honorable Axis disciples! My name is Aqua! Yes—Aqua, goddess of water, the very deity you revere! My sweet believers, I myself have come to rescue you!" she announced from the top of her box.

The crowd, which had been simply watching until that point, went dead silent.

"…Okay. Time to go. Quick, Megumin."

"…This will not do. I thought perhaps this situation could be resolved until a moment ago, but I was wrong. Let us get out of here!"

"W-wait! Mr. Kazuma? Miss Megumin? What about Lady Aqua and Miss Darkness…?"

As Megumin and I started sneaking away, a wave of taunts rose from the crowd.

"Pshaw! What a scoundrel!"

"Sure, she has blue hair and blue eyes—but the gods still won't be happy that she's pretending to be Our Lady Aqua."

"Throw her in the lake! If she's really the goddess of water, she won't mind!"

"Waaaah! Stop! It's true! I really am a goddess!"

"Oh! R-rocks…! St-stop throwi—! Aqua, get behind me…!"

"".........""

"Hey, where are you two going…?" Wiz asked. "Lady Aqua is…!"

As the crowd began to stone Aqua and Darkness, Megumin and I made our escape.

We took the long way around to get back to our hotel. By the time we arrived, Aqua was already there.

"Waaaaaaahhh!!"

Apparently, she had been crying the entire time. Had she even *stopped* crying since she arrived?

"L-Lady Aqua, here's some warm milk. Have a sip and t-try to calm down a little…"

Wiz was trying to comfort the weeping Aqua in the middle of the big room where the girls were staying.

Nearby, Darkness was contentedly sipping some black tea, somehow looking refreshed despite all the scratches and cuts covering her.

They had been stoned and ridiculed—one more reason for our pervert to love this town.

Maybe we should just leave her here.

"It's too muuuuch! I'm trying so hard to help everybody! How could my own followers throw rocks at me?! Waaaaah!"

"Lady Aqua, p-please calm down! Your holy power gets stronger when you're agitated, and I might start to disappear...!"

A frantic Wiz was trying to offer some hot milk to Aqua. She glanced at it and sniffled.

"...I want wine."

"You aren't actually that upset, are you?"

Aqua looked up at me, her face a little clearer now that Wiz had shuffled downstairs to get some alcohol.

"That doesn't matter. There is definitely a plan afoot to destroy this town. Several of the hot springs I visited were very polluted. If any guests had gotten in those, they would have gotten sick or worse."

"Aqua," Darkness said, "I trust your skills as a priest if nothing else, and if you're so insistent about this, I'm sure it's true. But if you can't even say who did it, what's the use?"

"She is right," Megumin said. "Why not just report it to the Adventurers Guild or the manager of the hot springs and let them handle it?"

At that, Aqua ground her teeth in frustration. This involved the Axis Church, and she probably wanted to handle it herself.

I knew how she felt about her followers, but given how they had just treated her, why bother saving them?

"Oooh... But if this goes on, my sweet little followers will...!"

Aqua clung to one end of the table, teary-eyed.

Sigh. *I guess I've got no choice...*

"Tomorrow, I'll help you out. But we have to avoid anything that might turn into an actual battle, okay? Once we find the perp, we leave the rest to the Adventurers Guild. Got that?"

She was positively ecstatic.

5

"All right, I'll just stay here. The rest of you, be safe!"

The next morning...

Wiz said good-bye to us as we left for the city's Adventurers Guild.

We were leaving her at the hotel as a point of contact.

Our plan was to split up to gather information and let one another know if we found anything. That meant we would need some way to get in touch. So with Wiz at the hotel, the four of us made for the hot springs.

"I don't know," I said. "I wonder what we're going to do about this criminal. Even if we do spot someone suspicious, we can hardly have him arrested unless we actually catch him poisoning a bath or something."

Not that I didn't have a good guess as to who was behind it.

It had to be that tan brown-haired man who was at our hotel.

Since our chance encounter earlier, I had seen neither hide nor hair of either the woman or the man anywhere.

The woman had said she couldn't relax in the baths here anymore, so maybe she'd skipped town. Which possibly meant the man was acting on his own now...

"Heh-heh-heh! Just leave it to me. As a matter of fact, I've already put a plan in motion to catch the criminal! How's this? Our target has to enter the baths several times a day, right? After all, the best way to poison a bath would be to go in as a regular customer."

Wow, Aqua was actually using her head for once. She puffed out her chest as she spoke.

"So I went around with a survey, asking the owners of a number of hot springs to recall what kind of customers had come by."

"Gosh, you've really gone above and beyond this time…"

Maybe this was really how much she cared about her followers. I wished she would exert this sort of effort all the time.

"I see. Not even tourists and aficionados would visit that many hot springs in a single day. This will allow us to narrow it down to the people who were seen at the most baths." Megumin, as usual, caught right on.

"And if somebody on that list left a lot of trouble behind him, that would be our guy." Darkness, too, sounded suitably impressed.

"Exactly! Now I just need to go to the places where I dropped off the survey and collect the results!"

Seriously. I wish she were like this every day.

I think all of us were surprised to see Aqua functioning so well.

We split up, each going to different hotels to find out the results of Aqua's questionnaire. Then we met up again in a public park and spread the sheets out on a bench to compare them.

"Okay, the results are in!" Aqua said. "The person seen at the most hot springs was…"

A woman with light-blue hair and eyes, wearing a light-purple feather mantle.

"So you were the culprit all along," I quipped.

"Was not! Just hold on. Yes, I went to a lot of hot springs, but that was to purify them! Look at the responses from the hotels where there were problems. They must mention who the last person was to go in before the trouble started—that person is the most suspicious!"

As Aqua instructed, we checked the surveys from the affected hotels to find the last visitor to each one.

A woman with light-blue hair and eyes kept turning the hot springs into regular hot water as a prank…

*   *   *

"…That's you again."

"I don't get it! Why is this happening?! This didn't help at all!"

"Wait, hold on a moment." Megumin stopped the sniffling Aqua, who was on the verge of shredding the questionnaires. She picked up the papers with an unusually serious look.

"See this? '**A man with short brown hair and tan skin.**' After Aqua, he was the most frequently sighted person. Are men usually this interested in bathing?"

Huh. Well, I guess the Crimson Magic Clan was renowned for its intelligence, if nothing else.

"So I guess he's our man," I said, taking the questionnaires from Megumin and trying to affect nonchalance. "Muscular, tall…"

"…Hey, hang on a second," Aqua said. "Why do you guess that? How would you know? Kazuma… Could it be? Even though you're always acting mad at me, you were actually so worried that you were quietly investigating to make sure I was all right? Really? Don't tell me you're one of those hot-cold types?!"

Her eyes were sparkling, and she seemed genuinely keen to hear the answer.

"Nah. I happened to overhear him in the bath the day we got here. 'Now that awful sect is done for. Our plot to destroy their precious bath is done. Right now, everything is going to plan at the other places, too. If all goes well, we need only wait. We're long-lived—what's ten or twenty years to us?' You know, something like that. Just… Yikes! Grrgh! What are you doing?!"

Aqua was suddenly strangling me.

"That's *important*! Why didn't you say something sooner?! If you had told me about that right away, I could have skipped all this work!"

"Hey, stoppit already! We came here to relax, didn't we? Why does every single thing we do have to end up with us risking our lives?! It was obviously going to turn into a huge pain in the neck, and I didn't want to go out of my way to get dragged into it!"

"Listen to you! Have you no pride as an adventurer?! This is obviously an evil plot by the Demon King, isn't it?!"

"You trash! Aqua, I'll hold him down—you punch!" Darkness hollered.

"H-hey, stop! Stoppit! You really wanna go? Don't underestimate me…!"

6

"Erg… Awful… To think the tables could've been turned so thoroughly," Megumin said from where she rode on my back. I had stolen all her MP with my Drain Touch, and she sounded at once exhausted and envious.

"What a good-for-nothing guy…" Darkness sounded equally tired, her face covered in mud courtesy of Create Earth and Create Water.

Aqua, her hair frozen in places, stood in front of us and held out a sheet of paper.

We had finally arrived at the Adventurers Guild. Based on her questionnaire and my report, Aqua had drawn a photorealistic portrait of our target. We had come here to ask for help catching the guy, but…

"I understand, but, ma'am, the only evidence you have is something you claim to have overheard by chance. That's not much to arrest someone on. It might be one thing if you were adventurers of long standing in this town, but we barely know who you are. We can hardly just take your word on it. You'll have to bring some more convincing proof…"

The receptionist at the Guild was not buying our story.

No surprises there, given a bunch of strangers just appeared all of a sudden and said, "Arrest this guy."

Aqua, however, leaned in close to the Guild employee.

"Hey! If you live in this town, that means you're an Axis disciple, right? I want you to look closely at my face. Does it look familiar from anywhere?"

"...? I'm not actually part of the Axis Church, but now that you mention it, I do feel like I've... Oh! In the amusement district! You were the backup dancer at that one shop, right?"

"What?! No! As if I'd ever work at a nasty place like that—as the *backup*, no less!"

I couldn't quite follow Aqua's train of thought, but something suddenly occurred to me.

Our self-proclaimed goddess couldn't get herself recognized in a town that was supposed to be packed with her own followers. But we had someone even more famous with us.

"Hey, Megumin, play along with me for a moment."

"Play along? What do you mean?"

As I spoke, I transferred enough MP to Megumin that she could stand on her own. She slid off my back with a perplexed expression, and I gave Darkness a little push forward.

"Do you know who stands before you?" I asked. "This is the honored daughter of 'the kingdom's confidant,' the great Dustiness family! Her Ladyship Lalatina Ford Dustiness! Hardly some mere unknown adventurer!"

""What?!""

Darkness seemed every bit as surprised as the receptionist.

Megumin figured out immediately what was going on and stood tall next to Darkness.

"Now, Young Lady. Show this hardheaded employee the proof of your status!"

"Huh?! Megumin, you too?! Ergh... I'm not so sure about bringing my family's reputation into this..."

Darkness didn't really want to make use of her rights as a noble, cringing as she pulled out her pendant.

It was the same one she had brought out during my trial. And it had the same effect any famous character has when they suddenly reveal their true identity.

"Th-that pendant! I-I-I'm very sorry! I'll have this man arrested immediately!"

The necklace had an instantaneous, almost theatrical effect as the receptionist hurriedly snatched the picture from Aqua.

"Way to go, Darkness! That's how to throw your noble weight around!"

"A-Aqua! Keep your voice down when you say things like that!"

"A-all right! In accordance with your honorable instructions, we've taken careful note of this man. If anything develops, we'll contact you at your hotel."

"Th-thanks. Let us know how it goes."

The employee bowed to us repeatedly as we left the Guild. Darkness shrank apologetically.

From behind her, I called, "Oh, by the way. I hope the Dustiness family can pick up the tab on our expenses here."

"?!"

7

We had finished all the necessary paperwork and were heading back to our hotel.

"You stinking—! You obnoxious—!"

Darkness was still angry.

"Aww, what now? I'm sorry, already! Fine, if it'll make you feel better, we'll have Aqua pay all the fees for the paperwork."

"What?! Why me?"

"That's not the issue! You can't just go throwing around my family's name whenever you want...!"

"Hey, Aqua. Darkness's family has enough trouble raising a prodigal daughter. Throw them a bone. Think of it as the fee for saving your church."

"Aww… Fine. I get it. I know how rough Darkness's family has it. I'll pay."

"Grraaaahhh…!!"

"Yikes! Wh-what the hell? Stop it!"

I dodged Darkness's sudden attack and then took up a stance from which I might be able to reciprocate.

"Gosh, what are you two making such a fuss about? People are watching, you know," said Megumin. "And, Darkness, I suppose you are a noblewoman, as far as it goes. Show a little restraint…"

"'As far as it goes,' my foot! I *am* a noblewoman. Sheesh…!"

She seemed totally exhausted for some reason, and I threw a few empty punches in her direction. "You remember how you were, like, no help at all with Destroyer? Well, here's your chance to protect some citizens like a good noble should."

"Whatever! You've done nothing but make fun of me this whole time!"

"Oops, what a lackluster attack! You couldn't hit me if I were standing still!"

"Hit you? I'll kill you!"

"Again I say, calm down! People are looking at us!" Thus it was Megumin who finally talked Darkness down from her fury over my taunts.

"Geez. You'd think knowing I was nobility might change your attitude toward me a little bit, but noooo…" Her annoyance was plain. But under her breath, she added, "People tell you they don't care, but everyone's a little wary around you when they find out…"

She sounded almost glad that we didn't treat her differently now that we knew.

"Noble or not, you are still Darkness. Why should our attitudes change? And anyway, the Crimson Magic Clan pays no heed to station. We will speak our mind to any noble or king."

"Megumin…"

"In my country, people complained about politicians all the time. And personally, I don't care about social status or even gender. So I'd sure never feel obligated to fawn over a noble who's barely making ends meet like you."

"K-Kazuma, you too? …Wait a second, what was that about barely making ends meet?" She snatched me by the collar with a glower.

I ignored her, instead looking to the last member of our party. "Come on, Aqua. Say your part. Tell her you'll never let status come between us or whatever… Hey, what's that you're making…?"

I trailed off as I saw Aqua deftly creating something as we walked along.

Was that clay she was holding? Where had she been keeping it?

Wherever it had come from, she was completely absorbed in making a sculpture from it.

"This? …Oh, I'm just copying Darkness's pendant from earlier. Here, look. Can't tell the difference, can you? With this, we can pretend to be members of Darkness's family and get anything we want… Oh noooo!"

Darkness seized the lump of clay and flung it away.

"Welcome back! How did it go?"

Having returned to the hotel, we filled Wiz in on the details.

We'd given the information on our suspect to the Guild and then made sure every bathhouse in town got a copy of it, so there was nothing else we could do.

The guy would probably be careful about going to any of the hot springs, and we couldn't very well just hang around town. In the end, we decided to do what we had come here for in the first place: enjoy the baths.

"It was an awful lot of work. But I'm glad we were able to stop the Demon King's plans before anything happened… Hey, Darkness. You're a sheltered noble, so you probably don't know this, but among the common folk, when guys and girls go on a trip, it's tradition for them to bathe together at least once. We're leaving tomorrow, so we'd better hurry up and keep the custom."

"?! I-I've never heard of a practice like that!"

"Like I said, it's something the lower classes do. You nobles wouldn't know about it. If you really want to bridge the gap between our status and yours, now's the perfect chance."

"Is—is that a real custom...?"

"No, it is not," Megumin interjected.

Just as I was dodging an attack from a red-faced Darkness, we heard an urgent knock.

"Yes, who is it?"

Aqua opened the door to find the employee from the Adventurers Guild clearly out of breath, presumably from running here.

"Wh-what's going on?" I asked with rising unease.

"It's terrible! The hot springs...! Every hot spring in town is suddenly welling up with poisoned water...!"

Chapter 5

May There Be a Goddess for This Impure Town!

1

It was the morning after we'd learned that every hot spring in town had been poisoned. After breakfast, we gathered in the girls' room.

"I'm concerned about the main springs," said Aqua, who had spent the previous day going around purifying the baths.

Apparently, the poisoned water had appeared only briefly and then stopped flowing—almost like someone was doing an experiment.

No sooner had Aqua heard the Guild employee's report than she made a beeline for town and started decontaminating everything she could get her hands on.

"The main springs? Those are in those mountains behind the Axis Church, aren't they?"

Aqua nodded.

Behind the huge church, home to the Axis sect, were the water sources widely regarded as the town's lifeline. Naturally, they were very carefully guarded, and I couldn't imagine they would be easy to sneak into.

"True, I doubt someone could go from bath to bath in such a short time. Our spreading that information around must have made him anxious, and he decided to attack the source directly, no matter the consequences. That seems the most obvious theory."

It would certainly be quicker to poison the wellsprings than every individual bath.

"But the question would be how he got in to such a carefully guarded location," Wiz said, knitting her brow.

"Kazuma," Darkness broke in, "what is that you've been eating? Let me try some." She grabbed my snack—something that looked a bit like pizza and passed for junk food in this world.

. . . .

"You know you've been looking even dumber than Aqua these days?"

"?!"

Darkness dropped the pizza gracelessly before it even got to her mouth. Her face was stiff with shock.

"Excuse me," Aqua interjected, "but that makes it sound like you think I set the standard for dumbness around here."

"Well, you do... Hey, stoppit! I take it back—I apologize. You've worked really hard on this trip and even used your head a little! I'm sorry, so give me back my pizza!"

As I had it out with Aqua over my food, Darkness stood up suddenly.

"...The source, right? Well, Kazuma, don't just sit there; let's go! We're going to head to those mountains and find out what's going on!"

She seemed awfully invested in this. Maybe she was frustrated feeling like all she could do to help was tout her family's name.

"Okay, sure. Let's see what the deal is with this water source."

2

Just to the left of the massive church that was the Axis headquarters, there was an enormous lake that served as the source for all the town's water.

And behind the church were the mountains the water flowed from.

A division of knights from the town was strictly guarding the path leading to the spring.

"Come on, I'm an Arch-priest of the Axis Church! Here, look at this! Hey, you're not looking!"

Aqua was trying to foist her Adventurer's Card on one of the guards. We had been stopped at the entrance to the mountains.

"I understand that, but you still can't come in here."

"Yeah, only the hot-springs manager is allowed."

The guard didn't even bother glancing at Aqua's card, despite her attempts at persuasion. The two knights didn't have to voice their suspicions; we could feel it.

Both of them were outfitted in full armor, on the off chance that anyone tried to muscle through. No way were they going to let a bunch of ragtag adventurers go up the mountain just because they'd shown up out of nowhere and asked.

"O my beloved Axis disciples… Listen well, for this thing is needful and right. Let us through, and this town will be—"

""Oh,"" they both replied, ""we're Eris followers.""

"Whaaat?! How can you follow Eris when you live *here*?! Come on, pleeease? Let us through! The main springs are in danger! This is for everyone's sake! I…I just want to save this town!"

She clung to one of the guards, weeping.

I had an idea, but I was kind of enjoying the show, so I thought I'd let it play out a little longer.

"Rules are rules! Now, go home!"

"Oh! Wait! You're kind of— You know, you're awfully handsome. Your profile reminds me of a…a Red Dragon!"

"Are you calling me lizard-faced?"

Since cajoling didn't work, apparently flattery was now her tactic of choice.

"…Fine. If you really won't let me through, I'll go to that church back there all weepy and tell them the nasty old Eris followers up here said super-mean things to me!"

"That's the dumbest thing I've ever heard!"

"Geez, this is why no one likes Axis followers! What's with that blue hair and those blue eyes, anyway? You look an awful lot like the person who went around turning all the hot springs to hot water yesterday…!"

"N-no! Th-that was… I was purifying them!"

"So it *was* you! One more reason not to let you through. Get out of here; go home!"

Now she was trying threats, but the guards simply shooed her away.

"I figured this would happen. Come on, Darkness, you may not get a lot of chances to help out, but this is one of them."

"Not a lot of chances?! I help out all the time— Hey, don't push me!"

Megumin, standing next to me, had already figured out what I was up to.

"Do you know whose presence you stand in?! This is Miss Lalatina Ford Dustiness of the great and famous Dustiness family! This is an emergency—the fate of the town hangs in the balance!"

""What?!""

"Yes! Consider this an order from the Dustiness family. After yesterday's commotion about the poisoning of the hot springs, it was much more reasonable to think that someone poisoned the water source rather than every individual bath. We have come here to investigate on the Young Lady's instructions."

We shoved Darkness forward, where she held fast to the pendant around her neck.

"I agree it's an emergency, but I still don't know about using…"

Darkness was trying to say something, but we had her pinioned.

"Go on, Young Lady, prove it to them with that pendant you're hiding. Please, there's no need…to…resist… Young—! God, just do it already, Young Lady!"

"Kazuma, hold her tight! I'll— Ouch! Darkness, that hurt! Wiz! Megumiiin! Quick, take it from her! Grab that pendant!"

"Wiz, hold her right arm! And, Aqua, you take the left! Young Lady, resistance is…futile…!"

"I'm sorry! Miss Darkness, I'm so sorry!"

"Stoppit, you—! The Dustiness family name shall not be used to— Huh?!"

Megumin finally succeeded in prying the pendant from her and showed it to the guards. "How about that?! Surely you will let us through now!"

"O-our apologies!"

"We're very sorry. Please forgive our disrespect!"

Megumin seemed pleased by this change in tone as the two guards scrambled to make way for us. "…Could I borrow this for a bit?"

"Of course not. Give it back!"

Megumin deflated as Darkness grabbed the pendant from her.

—As this was happening, the guards came squirming back up to us.

"Ahem, L-Lady Dustiness, you said you are here to have a look at the water source, but truth be told, the person responsible for the main springs is already up there."

"We were given strict orders not to let anyone through while he was doing his inspection…"

We all looked at one another.

Now, of all times?

Maybe the manager or whoever had also decided the source must have been poisoned.

…Just to be sure, I asked the knights, "Did the guy who went up there happen to be kind of tan, with short brown hair?"

"No, an elderly man with golden hair. He has taken care of these wellsprings for a very long time."

My mistake… But then, where in the world did the brown-haired man go?

He wasn't easy to miss, and we'd made sure every hotel in town had his description. Somebody ought to have seen something by now.

"And there are monsters in these mountains. Lady Dustiness, if you insist on going up there, please be careful."

3

We carefully worked our way up the slope, which was overgrown with plant life and still had slippery snow in some places.

I'd pictured a mountain serving as a water source as a craggy, barren rock face, but here we were.

"Goodness, Miss Darkness! A member of the Dustiness family! Please pardon all the lapses of etiquette I've made!"

As we climbed, Wiz, who had been unaware of Darkness's noble background, kept bowing her head and saying things like that.

"No, Wiz, you go on treating me like you always have. That would be best for all of us."

"Are you sure? Well, if you say so, milady..."

She smiled. Darkness looked at her and sighed.

"That's exactly what a normal person would say... It's kind of comforting, somehow. It reminds me that the rest of my partners really are just disrespectful louts..."

Her face suggested some inner turmoil about all this as she went ahead of us, hacking a way through the bush.

"Well, you're a pain. Do you want to be treated like a noblewoman or like one of the gang? Make up your mind. Anyway, if you want us to treat you like nobility, you'll have to watch the way you talk when you get angry. And stop being so stubborn."

"A pain?! And, Kazuma, you're the one person in the world least qualified to criticize the way people talk! As I recall, you're younger than me. But you just talk the same way to everyone, including me..."

"That just shows that I think of you as a friend. Not Lalatina, the older noblewoman, but Darkness, the reliable Crusader."

"...I see... Well, in that case, I guess..."

She was blushing in embarrassment, her attitude much improved. As she began pushing forward again, I muttered, "Too easy."

"Easy indeed," Megumin agreed.

"Yep, easy!" Aqua echoed.

"Why— Why, all of you…!"

"…?"

Wiz looked back at us reprovingly, while Darkness walked ahead in high spirits.

"Seems like we've been walking a while," I said. "Didn't the guard say something about monsters around here? I hope the guy who came in before us is okay. Can an old man deal with whatever's up here?" I asked nonchalantly. As if in answer, the sound of a faraway fight reached our ears.

"Kazuma!" Aqua yelled. "That's what happens when you say stuff like that! It turns into a flag!"

"Idiot, I didn't—! I just asked a question…!"

"No fighting, both of you—let's just go!"

Wiz's urging sent us scrambling in the direction of the sound.

A strange sight met our eyes.

"Wh-what is that?" Megumin asked dumbly.

When we arrived, there was already no sign of the manager, but…

"Could this…be a Beginner's Bane?"

Darkness crept up to the black form, inspecting it closely.

A battle had occurred here, no question.

But it didn't look like any of the plant life had been cut with a sword or singed with magic. The only signs of the struggle were a dark pelt and a massive fang from a Beginner's Bane.

There wasn't much left of the body, almost as though it had been dissolved with acid or something…

"Wiz drove off that Beginner's Bane yesterday without much trouble, but normally it would take some midlevel adventurers to take one down, right?"

Everyone seemed to understand what I meant. Could a single elderly man have done this?

In other words…

"That old man must be really strong! Let's hurry up and find him and get him to protect us!" Aqua cried.

…Okay, so one person didn't understand what I meant.

"No old man is strong enough to defeat a Beginner's Bane by himself! This wasn't done by any human."

"Wh-what do you mean?" Aqua asked. "That middle-aged butcher in Axel hunts frogs and Fire Drakes on his own! Why can't there be an older guy who can fight a Beginner's Bane?"

"Those are small-fry compared with this! And look at the corpse. This isn't normal."

The way it had apparently melted was extremely strange. Could magic have done this? And if it could…what a nasty spell.

"Whatever the story is, we'll have to be careful. That isn't just any old man."

Everyone except Aqua nodded silently.

She, instead, muttered dejectedly, "There was a cook who once skewered a Brutal Alligator alive, they said…"

She just couldn't let it go.

4

We'd covered a respectable distance, but luckily, there was no mistaking the path. Six huge pipes ran down the side of the mountain to carry water from the wellsprings to the town, so if you wanted to reach the source, you just had to follow the pipes.

It took a lot of endurance to climb the snowy mountain, though. I checked on the rest of the party, figuring everyone must be tired…

"Hey, Wiz. You're a Lich, right? Don't you have some convenient Lich magic? Maybe flight or something?"

"Lady Aqua, there is no such thing as 'Lich magic.' I do have a few spells I developed on my own, but they're all for offensive use…"

"Oh-ho, developed on your own?" Megumin said. "I cannot let that comment pass. None of them happen to be more powerful than Explosion, do they?"

"Aww… I was pretty excited when he said there were monsters around here, but we haven't been attacked even once. What's with that…?" Darkness whined.

Everyone seemed perfectly perky.

"A-all right, everyone! L-let's slow the pace a bit, okay? If we run into any enemies, how—can we—fight them—if we're—out of breath?" I, for one, was already panting.

Aqua cocked her head at me. "…I knew your stats weren't very good, Kazuma, my friend, but I didn't think they were this bad."

Now, that hurt!

"What is your Vitality stat, anyway? If it turns out to be as low as an Arch-wizard's, I may not be able to look you in the eye again." Megumin sounded annoyed.

I couldn't speak as I showed Megumin my card, because I was still trying to catch my breath.

"……Well, you know. You've… You've got the lowest level here. Don't lose heart over it. You just need a few more levels."

Megumin pointedly averted her gaze from my card as she tried to comfort me.

"Hey, are you trying to say my stats really are as bad as yours?"

"Perhaps we should take a rest!" she called. "We have not caught up with the old man despite all our walking, and I think it would be better to be at full strength when we do find him."

"H-hey, do you mean my stats are even worse than yours? There's no way I have less Strength or HP than you do, right?!"

Megumin didn't answer but only plopped down where she was.

I…I need to raise my level…

After our break, we had set off walking again when we suddenly reached the end of one of the pipes. Just beyond, water was pouring out of the main spring, but…

Wait a second…

"Hey, this water is black!"

"?! This is poison! This is definitely poison!" Aqua cried and then shoved her hand straight into the polluted water.

"That's hot! Eeeeyow! It's boiling! It's burning me!"

"You idiot, why would you put your hand into the spring? Take your hand out!"

"B-b-but—! It's sooo hoooot!"

Aqua kept raising a ruckus but left her hand in the murky water.

I hurried up to her and intoned a magic spell in the direction of her hand.

"*Freeze!*"

It was just beginner magic, but it would cause the wellspring to turn to...

...Actually, it didn't turn to anything. My magic just wasn't strong enough.

"*Freeze!*"

Wiz rushed up and used the same spell.

Maybe it was the difference in magical power, or maybe because she was a Lich, but Wiz's spell immediately lowered the temperature of the water.

"Phew... Thanks, Wiz. And you, too, dear Kazuma. Thanks...kind of."

"What do you mean, kind of?"

Wiz continued casting Freeze on the water around Aqua's hand.

Slowly, the dark, cloudy water began to turn clear and clean.

"That will do it... But it's harder to purify what's already inside the pipe, so it'll take quite a while before this wellspring can be used again... *Heal!*"

Done purifying, Aqua healed the burns on her own hand, then gave a melancholy sniff, even though it was her own overexcitement that had gotten her into trouble.

The sight of her was even getting to me...

But anyway, now we knew for sure that someone had poisoned the wellspring. I couldn't say what the connection was between the manager and the man I had seen, but if we kept going, we would probably find out.

—Along the way, we saw that the wellsprings connected to each of the other pipes had been poisoned, too.

Aqua purified them one by one until she had taken care of four of the six sources.

But of course, it would take quite a while before they were fit for use again.

At length, we had probably come about 80 percent of the way up the mountain. I was just about ready to throw in the towel and go home when we caught sight of what seemed to be a human silhouette in the distance.

I looked closer with my Second Sight skill.

"…Huh? That's him, all right."

It wasn't the golden-haired old man the knights had told us about, but the man I had seen at the bath.

"What's up? Why'd you stop?"

Aqua was perplexed.

I pointed up ahead and told everyone our target was right there.

"Ah, I do see a human form," Darkness said. "I wonder what he's doing there. Does one of the main springs start there?"

"Perhaps," Megumin said. "Look, the pipe ends there… Wait, that must mean he's about to…!"

We had caught him in the act of polluting one of the springs!

We all rushed forward, and he finally noticed us. A strange expression came over his face as we approached.

"What are all of you doing? No one but the hot-springs manager is supposed to be allowed up the mountain. How did you get here?"

He sounded completely calm. Aqua leveled a finger at him.

"You're one to talk! How dare you try to make this city's baths unusable! Well, you're finished!"

"Unusable? I'm the one who watches out for these springs. I'm afraid you'll have to start talking sense…"

The man made a point of acting confused. Confounded, Aqua looked to me for help.

Well, don't rush in like that if you don't know what you're doing.

"Playing dumb will not help you," Megumin declared. "What are you doing here? Did you tire of poisoning individual hot springs and come to contaminate the source instead? Was the commotion yesterday to help you ascertain that the baths in town are connected to this water?"

"All the main springs on our way here were poisoned. As Megumin says—we will have an explanation from you of what you're doing here. I am Lalatina Ford Dustiness. By right of nobility, I shall take you to the police."

Megumin and Darkness closed in, but the man coolly cocked his head.

"I keep telling you, I don't know what you're talking about. Feel free to search everything I have with me. You'll find there's no poison of…any…kind…?"

He had started so confidently before trailing off. I followed his gaze…

"Hmm…? Who *are* you? You look very familiar…" Wiz had her hand to her chin and was staring intently at the man.

As soon as he noticed this, the man spun around as quickly as he could.

"A-anyway, I'm just here to investigate what all the fuss was about. So…"

"Oh! Mr. Hans! It's you, isn't it, Mr. Hans?!" Wiz exclaimed.

"H-Hans? Who's that? I'm…I'm the manager of the hot springs around here…"

"Mr. Hans! It's been ages! It's me, Wiz! The Lich?"

The man tried shakily to deny his identity under the barrage of *Hans*es, but Wiz was too caught up in seeing a familiar face.

Hans glanced at Wiz, who hadn't taken her eyes off him.

"A Lich? You mean one of those terrible undead monsters? I'm sure I don't understand a word you're saying. A-anyhow, you'll see I don't have any poison on me, so there's no proof of…"

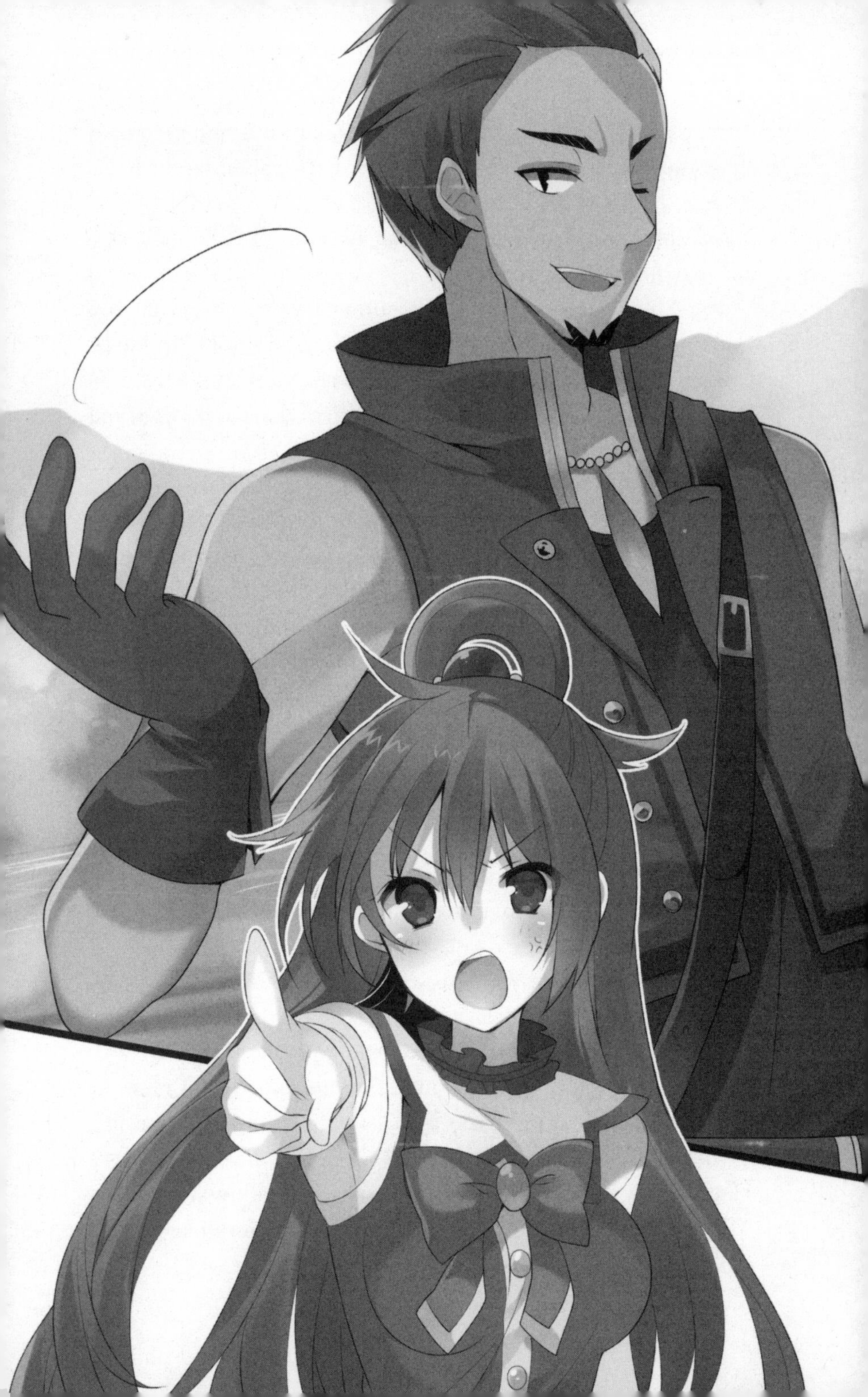

"Oh, speaking of poison! I vaguely recall you were a mutant form of Deadly Poison Slime, Mr. Hans. You haven't been poisoning the baths by any chance, have you?"

I don't think she even realized she had just annihilated his alibis.

She marched right up to Hans.

"Aww, Mr. Hans, why are you ignoring me? It's me, Wiz! You know, I remember you had a talent for imitation. Did you pretend to be the manager to get up here? Mr. Hans? Come on, Mr. Hans!"

"J-just you stop that! Who are you, anyway? I don't know you, and I've never— S-stop that. Let go of me! Please!"

Wiz had finally taken Hans by the shoulders and was giving him a good shake.

"Could you really have forgotten about me? You must remember me—you know, from the Demon King's castle?"

"Ahhhhhh—oh yes! I just remembered I have some urgent business to attend to! You know what? Upon careful inspection, I've figured out what was polluting the water source. I better hurry back to town, so… Could you… Could you let me through?"

"Just where do you think you're going, Hans?"

"As if we'd let you through, Hans!"

"Do you think your excuses will stand with us, Hans?"

Three girls stood blocking his way.

A frown came over Hans's face, and he took an involuntary step back.

"Enough games, Hans. Show us what you really are," I said.

"Hans this, Hans that! Don't you know better than to take someone's name so lightly? What the hell are you doing here anyway, Wiz? I thought you left the castle to set up a shop in some town. How are you gonna keep your store if you spend all your time at hot-springs resorts?"

Hans, finally showing his true colors, started berating Wiz.

"Th-that hurts! I am working, really! The more I work, the poorer I get, so I'm doing the best I can every day…!"

I wasn't sure Wiz's response made a whole lot of sense, but now wasn't the time to worry about that.

Hans gave a deep sigh and shook his head slowly.

"Haah... Now what? I've been studying this town and making preparations for ages, and I'm finally doing it... Wiz, as I recall, the only support you lend to the Demon King is in keeping up the barrier around his castle. And in return, the rest of us don't give you any trouble. So why are you bothering me?!"

"Whaaat?! Was—was I bothering you, Mr. Hans?! All I did was try to say hello to someone I hadn't seen in a long time..."

"That's bother enough! Look! Thanks to you, now they all know what I am!"

I still wasn't sure whether or not it had been intentional on Wiz's part. But Hans, his identity revealed, lowered his center of gravity in preparation for a fight.

"How about it, Wiz? Feel like having it out with me? Or will you just pretend you didn't see anything?"

Apparently, Hans was only really on guard against Wiz.

I guess that made sense. According to Wiz, this guy was a Deadly Poison Slime or something. That was a bit of a mouthful, but I guess it basically meant he was a variety of Slime. As a monster, probably not on the same level as a Lich.

And to think, when I'd first seen him in the bath, I had wondered if he might be some kind of boss character. But he was just a Slime.

"M-M-Mr. Hans, these people are my friends. And if this town loses its hot springs, it will have all kinds of trouble. Can't we...talk or something?"

She sounded almost apologetic. Hans laughed.

"Ha-ha! I knew becoming a Lich had made you soft, Wiz! When you were an Arch-wizard hunting us like dogs, you wouldn't have spared one minute for 'talk'!"

"Erk... B-back then, I didn't see as clearly..."

Wiz began to fidget from what appeared to be embarrassment.

It was hard to picture the sweet, friendly Wiz as a battle-hardened fighter.

When we got back, we would have to get Vanir to join us and share some stories about the old days.

And to that end...

"Hey, I hate to interrupt your little reunion, but are you about set? ...Hans, right? My name is Kazuma Satou. I helped take down Beldia, then led the operation that put an end to Mobile Fortress Destroyer, and just the other day I went toe to toe with the all-seeing demon Vanir."

It was time to mop this guy up and put all this trouble behind us.

"Wh-what?! A shrimp like you—?! I've seen children with better equipment than you, and you say you helped defeat Beldia *and* Vanir?"

All right, enough was enough.

"'Shrimp'? What a way to greet somebody. Whatever I look like to you, I've stared death in the face over and over."

"In fact, he's literally died over and over."

That was Aqua, tossing in an unnecessary comment from behind me.

"I knew you were an agent of the Demon King from the moment I saw you. And do you remember where that was? We've already met—in the mixed bath at a certain hotel!"

"...? Whaaat?! *You're* the man with that animal stare!"

A-animal? That was uncalled for.

"I heard what you two were saying that day. How you were planning to destroy the Axis Church! I knew you were both uneasy about me. That's why I kept staring at that huge-breasted woman you were with—to trick you!"

"Hey, where do you get off claiming that? You said you never mentioned this exactly because you wanted to avoid getting involved in any trouble," Darkness said behind me.

You know what? The peanut gallery has been awfully chatty today.

I noticed Hans starting to back up as I spoke.

He had been looking solely at Wiz until a moment ago, but now he seemed most concerned about me.

"I see you don't flinch, even knowing who you're confronted with. Maybe you aren't as fragile as you appear," Hans said, glaring at me.

Who I was confronted with? He was just a Slime, for crying out loud. Sure, he had transformed into a tough-looking human, but the fact of the matter was, he was a Slime.

Aka, the weakest monster in most kinds of games.

The name Deadly Poison suggested what his main attack probably was, but we had Aqua on our side, and she could get rid of poison.

Frankly, I didn't see how we could lose.

"Just be smart and give up. Wiz! You used to work with this guy, right? I know it might be hard for you to fight him, so just stay back."

"M-Mr. Kazuma, you're right that I'm not eager to fight him, but... Are you sure about this? Mr. Hans is..."

She fell back as I instructed, but she seemed to be trying to tell me something.

I drew my sword easily, the polished blade glinting in the light of the sun.

To think the first enemy I would test this fine new weapon on was a measly Slime.

Behind me, Aqua and the others took up stances, ready to join the fight at any time. Darkness stood next to me, holding her great sword directly in front of her.

"...I guess you're serious. Fine! It's been a while since a party of adventurers tried to take me down. All of them fled or begged for their lives when they saw my true form. Maybe you'll have a little more spine!"

Hans made a broad gesture. Why was he spouting off like he was a major boss or something?

"My name is Hans! General of the Demon King's army, mutant Deadly Poison Slime!"

He was acting like that wasn't a name you would hear just about... anywhere...

"...What did you just say?"

What had this Slime just said?

I could've sworn he said "general of the Demon King's army."

Wiz shouted from behind me. "Mr. Kazuma! Mr. Hans has an especially big bounty on his head, even for a general of the Demon King! Be careful! He's extremely strong!"

Great. Now she tells me.

I backed up, keeping my sword at the ready. I turned to Darkness.

"Hey, Darkness. Aren't Slimes supposed to be weak? They're just low-level monsters, right?"

Without letting her guard down for an instant, Darkness said, "Slimes? Weak? That's the stupidest thing I've ever heard. Some very small Slimes, maybe, but once they get big enough, they're serious enemies. For starters, physical attacks don't have much effect on them. They're strong against magic, and they'll eat anything and everything. If one gets ahold of you, it's essentially over. They'll reach your body through chinks in your armor and melt you with digestive juices or otherwise just block your mouth so you suffocate."

Man, that sounds scary. I mean... Wait, what?

Had I just unwittingly picked a fight with a major enemy?

"Kazuma, you must not touch a Deadly Poison Slime! And this one must have an especially lethal toxin if he is able to pollute every hot spring in town! Deadly enough to harm those who so much as get in the baths! If you were to come into direct contact with it, you would be killed instantly!"

"Killed...instantly...?"

Megumin's warning set my heart pounding.

"Not to worry, Kazuma! I can just bring you right back! As long as you don't get eaten, anyway. If he grabs you and dissolves you, even I won't be able to help!"

As did Aqua's.

"Now, brave adventurers, have at me! I think I'm going to enjoy... this...?"

I turned my back on Hans and started running as fast as I could.

5

I slid down the mountain, shoving through grass and bushes. Little branches beat at my face, leaving small wounds.

"Yaaaaah! Dear Kazumaaaa! Wait! Waiiit!"

"You idiot, hurry! Keep up, or I'll leave you behind!"

Oh man, oh man, oh man.

That guy was the most dangerous thing we'd run into yet!

If you touched him, you'd die. If he touched you, you would dissolve, and all the goddesses in the world couldn't bring you back.

"Aww… A Slime, huh…?"

Darkness almost sounded a little regretful, but Megumin held her hand and pulled her behind us.

Darkness, who had something of a fixation on monsters that could cover her in goop, had wanted to stay and fight Hans on her own, but of course we stopped her.

It wasn't that I didn't think she could handle his attacks, but when it came to hitting back, she would have been in a lot of trouble.

"M-Mr. Kazuma, you got out of breath so easily coming up this mountain, but you're quite quick at going down it…!" Wiz, at the tail of our formation, was doing her best to keep up.

And behind her…

"Are you taunting me, humans?! All that big talk, and now you're just going to run away? Aren't you adventurers? Aren't you ashamed?"

Hans, his face bright red, was hot on our trail.

"I'm an Adventurer, all right! The weakest class! So pardon me if I don't stick around to do battle with a general of the Demon King!"

"Weak, indeed! And yet you…! …What?"

Hans suddenly stopped dead.

Surprised, we slowed down a bit, too.

"You're an Adventurer? You mean capital *A*, supposed to be the lowest class—*that* kind of Adventurer? Not the common noun but the class like Arch-wizard or Priest?"

"Y-yeah, so what?"

Hans's eyes went wide for a moment, and then he closed them and let out a breath.

He acted awfully human for a Slime.

"I'll let you go, then. Now get lost, small fry!"

He spat out the words and turned up the road, heading back toward the water source.

"Phew. Well, I'm glad that's over."

"It's not over! Look, he's going back to the main spring!" Aqua was extremely unhappy, but frankly, that guy was just too dangerous.

"And what are we supposed to do about him? Even Wiz would have trouble handling him, and we don't know whether Darkness could even withstand his poison. Do you think a long-distance Ambush with Megumin's Explosion would do the trick?"

"Um...I think if you exploded Mr. Hans, the bits of his body would pollute this entire area. Slimes are strong against magic, so I think burning him up completely would be very difficult..."

It sounded like we were out of options.

"I'm not trying to sound self-important here, but even I can't think of anything this time. If he were susceptible to physical attacks, maybe I could have used my new sword..."

"Chunchunmaru's time will come. But it's true that that Slime will soon be able to do as he wishes with the wellspring."

"I told you not to call my beloved sword that. I sure as heck won't... I admit, though, we're pretty much through this time. Hey, Aqua, how about you just give up on this city's hot springs? Let them find a new industry to support themselves. Who really needs the Axis Church, anyway?"

I thought I was just being honest, but Aqua tried to strangle me regardless.

Even as I struggled with her, Hans was growing smaller and smaller in the distance.

Aqua looked up at him and made her opinion clear.

"Fine, then… Well! I'm going to purify that Slime if it kills me!"

And it was incredibly ill-advised.

6

When we caught up to Hans, he had his hand in the wellspring he'd been trying to poison before, one of the two he hadn't already contaminated.

Apparently, he had dispensed a lot of poison already; even from a distance, the water was dark and cloudy. Of course, that presumably included the water rushing through the pipe to town.

"Did it not occur to him to just destroy these pipes?"

I didn't understand why he would go to all the trouble of coming up here and poisoning the main springs.

I guess pipes could be repaired. But a poisoned wellspring might never be usable again. He was, in his own way, just playing it safe.

Maybe there weren't very many priests who could purify his deadly poison the way Aqua could.

"This pipe seems to be made of a magical metal. I don't think it would break so easily. It's the lifeline of this town, so I'm sure they did everything they could for it."

I nodded at Megumin, but Aqua, who had worked to purify the polluted springs, glared at us with impatience.

"Come on, could you act just a little more worried? This looks like serious trouble to me! I mean, if he poisons the last spring, all of this town's hot baths will become unusable! And then the whole Axis Church will fall apart!"

""""And what's (what is) wrong with that?"""""

"Waaaaah!"

At our collective response, Aqua clung to Wiz in tears.

"C-come on, everyone, stop teasing Lady Aqua! The point is, at this rate…"

I didn't think we were teasing, but whatever. Would it really be such a bad thing if that obnoxious sect went extinct?

"Oh, you're back. Well, we're down to one main spring, anyway. Once I poison it, I'll be finished with this town. Finally! Finally, I can say good-bye to this disgusting little city!"

I assume even generals of the Demon King aren't safe from the overtures of Axis followers when they're undercover in this town.

"Just how long have you been here?" I asked. "Hey... Come to think of it, you got up here by impersonating the manager, didn't you? What about the real manager? The old man with golden hair..."

"I ate him," Hans said, almost disinterestedly.

...Ate him?

"Wh-what did you say?"

"I said, I ate him. I'm a Slime. Eating is what we do. I had to eat him—"

Hans was about to say *in order to turn into him*, but...

"Cursed Crystal Prison."

A cold, quiet voice sounded around the snow-specked mountain.

"?!?!?!?! Yaaaaaaagh!!"

The spring that Hans was touching made a creaking sound and then instantly froze over.

Hans bellowed, his extremity trapped inside the spring.

I looked around to see who had cast the spell.

It was Wiz. At that moment she gave no hint of her usual warmth and instead looked every inch a Lich, the most powerful of the undead.

She gazed expressionlessly at Hans.

"As I recall, my neutrality toward His Majesty's army was contingent upon your doing no harm to those who did not specifically seek to fight you, as adventurers or knights might."

"Wiz! Stop this! Release me! Wiiiiz!"

She barely seemed to hear Hans's shouts.

"That adventurers may die in battle cannot be helped. As they support themselves by taking the lives of monsters, they should understand that one day their own lives may be forfeit. Knights are much the same. They collect taxes and protect the citizens in exchange. They receive compensation to risk their lives, and this, too, cannot be helped. However…"

"Wiz! Do you really want to fight me? If we use our full powers here, this entire area will pay the price…!"

Hans tried to get a word in edgewise, but Wiz was not having it.

"However, the manager of these hot springs did you no wrong."

Her accusation was quiet, and she wore a mournful look on her face.

I felt a tug on my sleeve.

I started and turned around to find Aqua and Megumin standing behind me.

…They must have been frightened by this unfamiliar, deadly serious Wiz.

I mean, I was, too.

Next to me, Darkness was in a low stance, perhaps getting ready to jump in and support Wiz at any time.

Dammit, if our sweet little Wiz could rise to the occasion like this, then so could I!

"Sorry, Wiz, but I'm not interested in fighting you. I'm just going to do what I came here to do and then go home," Hans said, and then as we watched, he tore off his own right arm.

The arm, still stuck in the ice, popped off easily, and in its place a new, translucent limb grew instead.

Leaving his old arm where it was, Hans set off for the last wellspring.

7

We ran after him.

You know what? I feel like I've been doing nothing but running all day. What happened to my nice, relaxing hot-springs vacation? I came here to heal up, not to do physical training!

"Oh, Kazuma! That Slime is really fast! Aren't Slimes supposed to be, you know, blobby and cute or kind of blubbery and slow?"

It sounded like Aqua had exactly the same image of Slimes as I did.

Come to think of it, how could a Slime even be sentient? Where was its brain?

"Mr. Hans! I won't let you go any farther! *Cursed Crystal Prison!*"

"?! Dammit! I never did get along with you!"

Wiz's spell had encased Hans's lower body in ice just ten yards or so from the last spring.

Slimes were supposed to be strong against magic, and this one was a mutant Slime that had become a general of the Demon King's army. For a spell to work so readily— Well, that was a Lich for you.

But…!

"You're too soft, Wiz! Let me show you something else I've got up my sleeve!"

He tore off his own right hand and flung it toward the main spring.

""""Oh no!"""""

Everyone except Hans and me raised a cry as the appendage traced a beautiful arc through the air directly toward the spring.

And what was I doing?

"*Deadeye!*"

I pulled out my bow and sniped Hans's hand out of the air.

"Whaaa—?!" His eyes widened with surprise as he looked first at me, then at the spring.

He ground his teeth and started tearing pieces off his frozen lower body and flinging them one after another toward the water.

Your ability to hit things with Deadeye depends on your Dexterity and Luck. But high as my Luck was, there were simply too many bits and pieces to shoot them all down.

"Aqua! What was that magic you used to make your Luck better when we were playing rock, paper, scissors? Use it on me now!"

"Huh?! R-right!"

If she could use that spell from when we were arguing over the seat in the carriage, it would temporarily drive up my Luck stat—call it magical doping!

"*Blessing*!"

"*Deadeye*!"

The moment I had the buff from Aqua, I let loose with an arrow of enhanced distance and accuracy.

One after another I fired them, my aim always true, shooting down more than a few of the bits of Hans in the air.

As they watched, everyone except Hans and me let out a sigh of relief.

"Wh-what the hell's going on?! Who can shoot like that?!"

Megumin's response to Hans's outburst was calm.

"Do not underestimate this man's Luck! Though his stats are lower than a mage's, we have seen him defeat more than one powerful enemy in contests of luck alone."

"Hey, if you're gonna praise me, do it right!"

With our foe partially trapped in ice, Megumin and I were so confident that we could stand to have that argument.

And maybe our confidence caused us to let our guard down just a little bit.

Hans, in absolute frustration, pulled yet another piece from his body and flung it...

"Kazuma, go ahead and shoot that down, please!"

Aqua, her hands on her hips, didn't sound the least bit concerned.

"Just leave it to...! ...Oh."

As I was about to fire my arrow, I noticed something.

"Huh? Kazuma, what's wrong?" Aqua asked, surprised.

With a *sploosh*, the bit of Hans's body fell into the water.

""""""Huh?"""""""

My companions and Hans let out a cry, and I replied.

"...I'm out of arrows."

"N-noooooo!"

Aqua dashed toward the last spring and reached for the water.

"Lady Aqua, you mustn't! Part of Mr. Hans's body is in there! This is on a different level from the poison you dealt with in the other springs!"

Aqua ignored Wiz, shoving her hand into the water.

"Ahhhhit'shot, it's hot! *Heal*! *Heal*! Wiz, do something! This is the last spring and the last pipe, and they're gonna be poisoned!"

"L-Lady Aqua—! ...*Light of Saber*!!"

Aqua shouted to Wiz despite her burns, using Heal to keep the pain at bay.

In response, Wiz threw a knife hand, using light magic to cut away a part of the polluted pipe. She cut away only the part carrying the poisoned water, a section that would take only a matter of days to repair.

But just as we were all feeling a flush of relief...

...the sound of something cracking apart came from Hans's direction.

"Kazuma! K-K-Kazuma...!"

Megumin sounded genuinely terrified. I looked over.

There was Hans—or rather, the Slime who had taken on the form we knew as Hans.

"Why...! What an amazing specimen of Slime! Damn! If only you weren't poisonous, I would take you home and make you my pet!"

This from Darkness. The Slime hadn't even touched her, and yet her brain had already dissolved.

The creature was bigger than our house.

"That thing is huge!"

8

The Slime had become vast and round, no longer any hint of a human shape about it. It swallowed up the trees nearby, absorbing them into its body.

"Oh crap, I guess Hans is done playing around! Wiz, do something about this guy! Freeze him again or something! Just do him in!" I gave a shout and started running to keep from being absorbed by the ever-expanding Hans.

"I don't have enough MP to freeze something that big all at once! I need to get more MP from someone...!"

She was looking to me for help, but who around here had MP to spare for her?

"Megumin! You're going to have to be our sacrificial lamb! I don't have nearly enough magic, and Aqua's power would destroy Wiz!"

"Me?! A-a-absolutely not! I'll use my Explosion to blow him into tiny little pieces!"

"No, don't!" Aqua shouted. "The whole mountain will get poisoned!"

There was a clanking sound as Darkness began removing her armor. *Huh?*

"What do you think you're doing? Why are you taking your...?"

"Armor won't make any difference against a Slime. They just slide in through the cracks. So I might as well get rid of it."

Now I was sure her brain was mush. Darkness kept stripping off armor until she stood there in her civilian clothes.

"And anyway, I like this armor. I just got it cleaned. No way I'm going to let it get melted." Then she threw aside her great sword, too.

Physical attacks were meaningless against a Slime. If a weapon wasn't going to be any use, why bother with the weight?

"Hey, what do you think you can do with no armor and no weapon? Run!"

I grabbed Darkness's hand and began pulling her away, but she pointed wordlessly in the direction of the wellspring.

There...

"Waaaaah! Kazumaaa! *Pleeease*, dear Kazumaaaaa!!"

There was Aqua, her hand still in the spring, weeping and shouting but making no attempt to flee in the face of the oncoming Slime.

"You moron, what are you doing?! Forget about that and get the hell out of there!"

"But—! But—! If I don't protect this water, my followers will—!"

Darkness stepped up as if to protect Aqua, who continued her purification even though the water was scalding her.

Wiz approached Aqua, too, pale-faced but resolute.

"Kazuma, what do we do?! We need one of your dirty little tricks, and we need it now!"

"H-hey, what do you mean, 'dirty little tricks'?! Dammit... Fine! I'll think of something. In the meantime, do whatever you can!"

"Wh-whatever I can?"

Megumin, gripping her staff with both hands, sounded uncertain.

"Yeah, and for you that means just one thing! Your job is to finish off the boss! Wait with the others once you're ready to use your magic!"

Megumin gave her staff an extra squeeze, and I left her there, making for Hans.

The splorching mound of black jelly wasn't content with eating up all the trees around us; it was starting to take in nearby hills as well.

Now that Hans had abandoned any pretense of a human form, maybe he was exercising his true powers. He made no attempt to attack us but headed lazily for the springs, consuming everything he encountered on the way.

With my weapons and skills, there wasn't anything I could do to the massive Slime.

So...what was I supposed to do?

I could try Freeze, but Hans probably wouldn't get so much as a coat of frost.

And because he was so close to the spring where Aqua and the others stood, we couldn't use Explosion even if we wanted to.

If Aqua would just give up and run away, that would help. The scaredy-cat had chosen a really inconvenient time to grow a backbone.

I was out of arrows, so I couldn't even try to draw Hans's attention.

...Hang on.

I figured Hans was essentially in his true form at this point. So if I used a certain something I had with me...

"Lady Aqua, even if I used every last drop of magic I had, I wouldn't be able to freeze something that size! I know you're doing this for the Axis Church, but think how much worse it would be for them if anything happened to you!"

"Noooooo! What will I do if I can't protect my followers? If I can't save their home, what good am I? Keep on Freezing, please!"

No matter how desperate Wiz's pleas as she cooled Aqua's hand, the goddess wouldn't be moved.

Beside them was Megumin, ready with her spell and waiting for my signal, and Darkness was cricking her neck in preparation for the fight.

At Darkness's feet were her beloved armor, her sword, and...

...all the souvenirs she and I had bought together.

"Darkness, grab that stuff on the ground and come over here!"

"Stuff? You mean these souvenirs?"

She obligingly ran over to me with the load of gifts. I took out of my bag the ones I'd been carrying: the Arcan buns and meat buns we had gotten from the round-eared elf and the beardless dwarf.

I began flinging them toward Hans.

"Aww! What are you doing?! Don't waste my buns! You'll pay for this, Kazu...ma..."

Darkness was incensed, but she trailed off when she saw what Hans did next.

He was eating the buns happily.

It made sense: Wouldn't a carb-rich, high-caloric snack be more appealing to a Slime than trees and dirt?

I took the mountain of gifts Darkness was holding.

"K-Kazuma, you can't! Those were for Father and the servants..."

I ignored Darkness, who seemed deliberately oblivious to what was going on, and began hurling the treats in the opposite direction from the main spring.

"You can always get more souvenirs! I'll even go get them with you! Don't look at me like that—just run!"

Darkness stopped looking pitiful just long enough to run back and join the others.

Hans seemed to have taken an interest in Darkness's snacks and was heading after them with a *splorch, splorch*.

"Wiz. If there was a little less of Hans—if he was everywhere at once—could you freeze him then?"

"I might be able to just manage it if he was half the size he is now..."

Only just, huh? ...All right.

"Aqua. Would you be able to purify the pieces of Hans as Wiz froze them?"

"Y-yes, I could! In fact, if this weren't such an emergency, I would show you what I can really do!"

I think this might actually work.

"And I protect everyone from any flying pieces, right?" Darkness said.

"You got it. We're counting on you."

For this, there was nothing we could do but trust Darkness's über-tough body.

Aqua had a holy item equipped that would protect her from status effects like poison. And Darkness was so sturdy that she might as well have been wearing a holy item. She could withstand even the poison of a general of the Demon King.

...Or so I hoped.

I was pretty sure she had said something about taking a bunch of skills that upped her resistance to status effects. Why have a defensive specialist along if not for situations like this? We would just have to trust her.

In front of us, Hans was still gleefully devouring the buns.

Magical attacks had barely any effect on him, and physical attacks, none.

If we touched him we would die of poison, and if we beat him, the entire area would be contaminated.

How do I keep getting into fights with these life-threatening boss monsters?

All I wanted was a nice hot-springs vacation.

I was starting to suspect I wasn't really so lucky after all.

"Kazuma, I am ready at any time! I have cooked up my best stuff!" Megumin had removed the patch from her eye, which was shining a bright crimson.

Hans had finished all the buns and was now looking for something new to eat. Or maybe obeying the last remaining bit of his rational mind.

Either way, he turned toward us.

I held my hand out to Wiz.

"When I give the signal, Wiz, take my magic. Just leave me enough to survive."

"What?!"

But even as she spoke, I was saying:

"...Okay, Megumin. Take it away. Do it!"

"Take it away, I shall! Here I go! *Explosion*!!"

Her magical blast tore into Hans, rending him into countless tiny pieces.

As Darkness moved to cover me, Wiz drained my magic as fast as she could, and I felt my consciousness growing dim.

I normally wasn't much for leaving my fate in the hands of these people. But this time, I would just have to trust my friends...

9

Several days later.

We, the heroes who had saved the town...

"*Sniff...* But I tried so hard... I really tried this time!"

...were headed back to Axel with a blubbering Aqua in tow.

"It is strange, but…in this case, I rather sympathize with you, Aqua…" Megumin tried to comfort her as the carriage bounced along.

But Aqua only gazed out the window and sniffled.

After we'd destroyed Hans…

Darkness had used her body to shield us from the rain of Slime bits while Wiz, brimming with the MP from me, had frozen all the pieces.

"…I wonder if Father and the servants will like these…," Darkness muttered, holding the new souvenirs she had bought.

I was getting some serious "daddy complex" vibes here.

But never mind her. I turned to Aqua.

"…You know, you don't have to go all out all the time."

"What was I supposed to do?! I thought if I didn't use all my strength, everything would be poisoned! Waaaaaaahh! I tried sooooo hard, and this is the thanks I get!"

I ignored Aqua as she kept sniveling and shifted my attention to Wiz, who still seemed a little drained. She was always pale, but now she was practically going to disa— *Hey, wait a minute!*

"Hey, she's disappearing! She's gonna vanish!"

"Darkness, she needs HP! Quick, give her some of your life!"

"O-okay! Kazuma, go!"

We flew into a panic inside the carriage trying to take care of Wiz.

I used Drain Touch to take some HP from Darkness, our toughest party member, and give it to the fading Lich. She started to return to normal, and we breathed a collective sigh of relief.

And somewhere in the middle of it all, Aqua, who was still looking out the window, shouted:

"I was just trying to purify everything! Why was everyone so upset?!"

We had gone to the Adventurers Guild to report the defeat of Hans, general of the Demon King's army, where we were greeted with more than a little gratitude for handling the troubles with the polluted water.

...Until the hot springs started running with nothing but regular old water.

After I had gone unconscious from loss of magic, Aqua had apparently started filtering in earnest.

As a result, the mountain spring, normally rich in minerals and other curatives, became nothing more than a gigantic pot of boiling water.

Not to mention, our long-suffering Lich nearly found herself in the next life thanks to the powerful purification.

Practically speaking, I guess you could say that Aqua was the one who finally fulfilled the Demon King's plan to cut off the source of the Axis Church's prosperity.

We had, in essence, destroyed the town's most important industry.

Normally, that would have meant a demand for a massive payment of damages.

But in this case, the Axis Arch-priest decided that since we did it to save the church, and since we had, in fact, prevented the town's actual destruction, much could be forgiven. We handed back the reward for Hans by way of compensation and got out of Dodge.

We had expected to simply go home by Teleport, but with Wiz still all but transparent, we wound up back in the carriage.

"Please, you have to listen to me! Both of you, why won't you listen?!"

"What is it you want? Let go—this carriage rocks quite enough without you shaking me, too."

"What is it? We'll listen. Go ahead."

Aqua regarded Megumin and Darkness with a somber expression.

"I think you understand that things turned out the way they did here because my power is too strong. I know you're dense, Darkness, and you're crazy, Megumin, but even you— Ow! Ow! H-hey, listen to me! What I'm trying to say is, even a couple of lugs like you must see the truth by now!"

Aqua tried to make her case with both Megumin and Darkness strangling her.

"I think it's about time you both believed I'm a real goddess!"

The other two fell silent for a moment at that.

"…Kazuma, we must find a place with more effective hot springs next time," Megumin suggested.

"Yeah. Specifically, effective on delusions," Darkness added.

"*Please* believe me!"

It was noisy inside the carriage.

But Aqua's renewed weeping was loudest of all.

Epilogue 1 —In the High Priest's Chamber—

"—That concludes my report on the recent events."

I scanned the written account I'd received and then let out a breath, trying to calm my pounding heart.

The priest who had brought me the report affected nonchalance, but I suspected that in his heart he, like me, was nearly mad with happiness. Earlier, he had periodically squeezed his eyes shut and whispered a word of thanks.

"A single person purified all the hot springs in town. To say nothing of the main springs, allegedly poisoned by the Demon King's general Hans, as well as the pieces of that general after he was defeated."

He had barely been able to contain the trembling in his voice as he read out the report.

"If we had gathered a score of our best priests, we might—*might*—have been able to cleanse the pieces of Hans after months of work."

"Yes, sir. And...that person's appearance..." The priest's voice quaked with emotion.

"Light-blue hair and eyes. A feather mantle. And according to the report, strikingly beautiful."

There was no mistaking her.

The thought of it nearly overwhelmed me with joy.

"What do you intend to do? The city's believers, shall we...?"

"Tell them? Yes, absolutely. But only with great care. You never know if she may visit again someday. In such an event, we must warn people not to mob her or speak to her at random. What is the current status of the baths she purified?"

"Their special qualities have been obviated, sir. However..."

"I hear people who have bathed in them have found their injuries healed, and that their water has the effect of holy water when used against undead."

"Yes, sir. Exceedingly strong holy water, at that... If I may be so bold, I believe bringing these products to market could be far more profitable than the hot springs ever were."

Well, naturally.

That most august personage put all her power into this act of purification—who could expect any less from it?

"...On that note. I regretted to hear that we seem to have demanded quite a sum in damages from them..."

"What shall we do, sir...? If we give no hint that we are aware of her true identity, she may be less concerned about returning here..."

"...Yes, perhaps you're right. Truth be told, I dearly wish to thank her for saving our town and to offer her my profuse apologies for demanding payment..."

But let that be for another time, when she came to our town once again.

The priest bowed deeply to me.

"Then if that is how you wish to proceed, Father Zesta..."

"I do. Please see to it."

He bowed again and left.

I read through the report once more with profound gratitude.

"On behalf of my entire church, I thank you from the depths of my heart—my lady Aqua!"

Epilogue 2 —At Journey's End—

"'Kay, baaack!"

"Can't you say 'We're home' like a normal person?"

Aqua came bounding into the house as I opened the door.

Let's take stock of this so-called vacation.

As usual, we got dragged into a bunch of good-for-nothing goings-on. Just remembering it made me feel a bit faint.

On the other hand, I did get to spend some time in a hot spring and even a mixed bath…

A mixed bath…

Then again, did I really? It was just that one time with that Wolbach chick. And she was careful not to let her towel slip.

Whereas at home, I'd gotten in the tub with Megumin and had Darkness wash my back.

……Wait a second. What?

Do I actually come out better when I stay home?

What gives?

"What's up? Is this a new game? 'Try to put on the dumbest smile you can'?"

"I was trying to do an impression of you. Pretty good, huh?"

Aqua sniped at me, and I responded in kind.

"Oh, give it a rest. We just got home. I'm going to go put on some tea. You two try to calm down," Darkness said as she took off her armor and went to wash her hands.

"Ahhh, there really is no place like home. Never mind that I was the one who suggested we go on vacation in the first place." Megumin flopped down on the sofa as she spoke.

"Wait a second, Megumin! I have dibs on that spot!"

"If you want this seat, then play me for it," Megumin said, pulling out a board game she was especially good at and starting in on it with Aqua.

I seated myself on the other end of the couch and watched the game. After a while, Darkness returned with the tea.

She doesn't usually show these kinds of domestic skills. Who knew she could make tea?

"Hey, Megumin," said Aqua. "Your Arch-wizard is a total thorn in my side. I have a Crusader here that I don't need. Wanna trade pieces?"

"My battle plan also has no need for a Crusader, so I am afraid I cannot trade. Come on, Aqua, it's your turn."

"Hey, I know you two are talking about the game, but…"

I let the conversation wash over me as I sipped my tea.

Maybe it was because we'd just gotten back from a trip, but I really appreciated the laid-back atmosphere.

But if things were going well and I was feeling good, that meant something was bound to happen.

I was learning.

"Megumin! Hey, Megumin, are you there?! And Mr. Kazuma?"

A knock on the door accompanied the desperate shout.

Aaaaand there it is.

"Yeah, we're here. Is that you, Yunyun? You in trouble or something? We can handle anything these days—Demon King minions, bounty heads…"

Yunyun was clearly surprised by this remark as I opened the door.

She was red-faced and agitated. Her shoulders heaved with her breath. I wondered what in the world had happened.

"Uh… Um…I know this is very sudden, but…"

She pursed her lips as if steeling her resolve.

I watched her, lazily drinking my tea.

Nothing could scare me anymore. Whatever was going on here, I would take it in stride.

"What is the matter, Yunyun? Did you want something with me?" Megumin stood up, but Yunyun gave a small shake of her head.

Then she looked straight at me.

Was this something to do with me? Whatever it was, I would handle it.

Yunyun watched as I calmly took a mouthful of tea.

"Mr. Kazuma! I...! I...!! I want to have your children!"

I spat out my drink.

FIN.

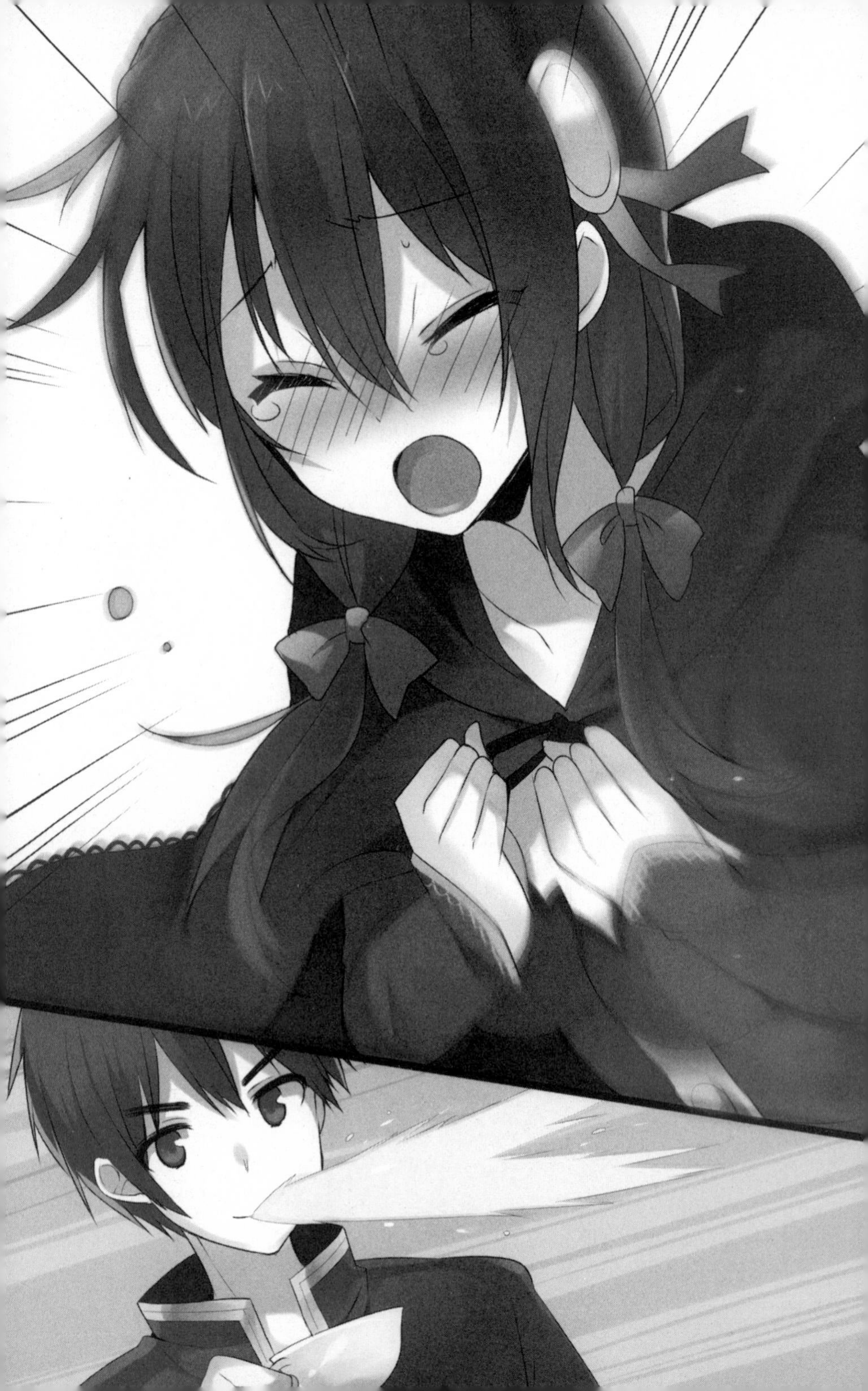

Hooray! It's Volume 4!

We've made it up to four volumes. Four books is enough that if you tied them all together in a block, you could hit someone with it and do some real damage.

Please kindly recommend this series to anyone seeking an effective weapon.

And even better, you can enjoy reading this weapon when you have some downtime.

First, some updates.

An Explosion on This Wonderful World!, currently being serialized on Sneaker Bunko's official homepage, The SneaWEB, is slated to be released in book form.

I'll be adding an entirely new chapter and a number of other little bits.

People who have been reading the spin-off may have noticed, but with this volume the two stories start to converge, so look forward to seeing that trend develop.

Moving on.

Amazingly, I'm told this series is going to be turned into a manga in *Monthly Dragon Age*!

A manga? Really? Incredible...! I'm practically shaking...!

Planning for the manga version is already underway. I hope you'll add it to the list of things you're looking forward to!

Starting around the next volume, I think it will be about time to trim the fat and pick up the pace. Maybe.

I'm sure you'll enjoy it, and I know I for one will be dancing around my garden with joy if you read it.

And with that, we've come safely to the end of another volume.

To the editorial staff, my editor K-san, everyone who was involved with designing and producing this book, the businesspeople, the bookstore people, and of course Kurone Mishima, my beloved illustrator.

I know I say this every time, but I can't find the words to express my gratitude. Thank you all so much.

And above all, thank *you*, dear reader, for picking up this book. Thank you from the bottom of my heart!

Natsume Akatsuki

NEXT

I want to have your children!

I'm on it!

...H-have you lost your mind?! Yunyun!!

What *is* she going on about?

...Is this some kind of high-level "pregnancy play"?

All right, all right... Aha, I get it. No need to be jealous.

....

A-anyway, come back to Crimson Magic Village with me!

KONOSUBA: GOD'S BLESSING ON THIS **WONDERFUL WORLD!** 5

Crimson Magic Clan, Let's & Go!!

COMING SOON!!

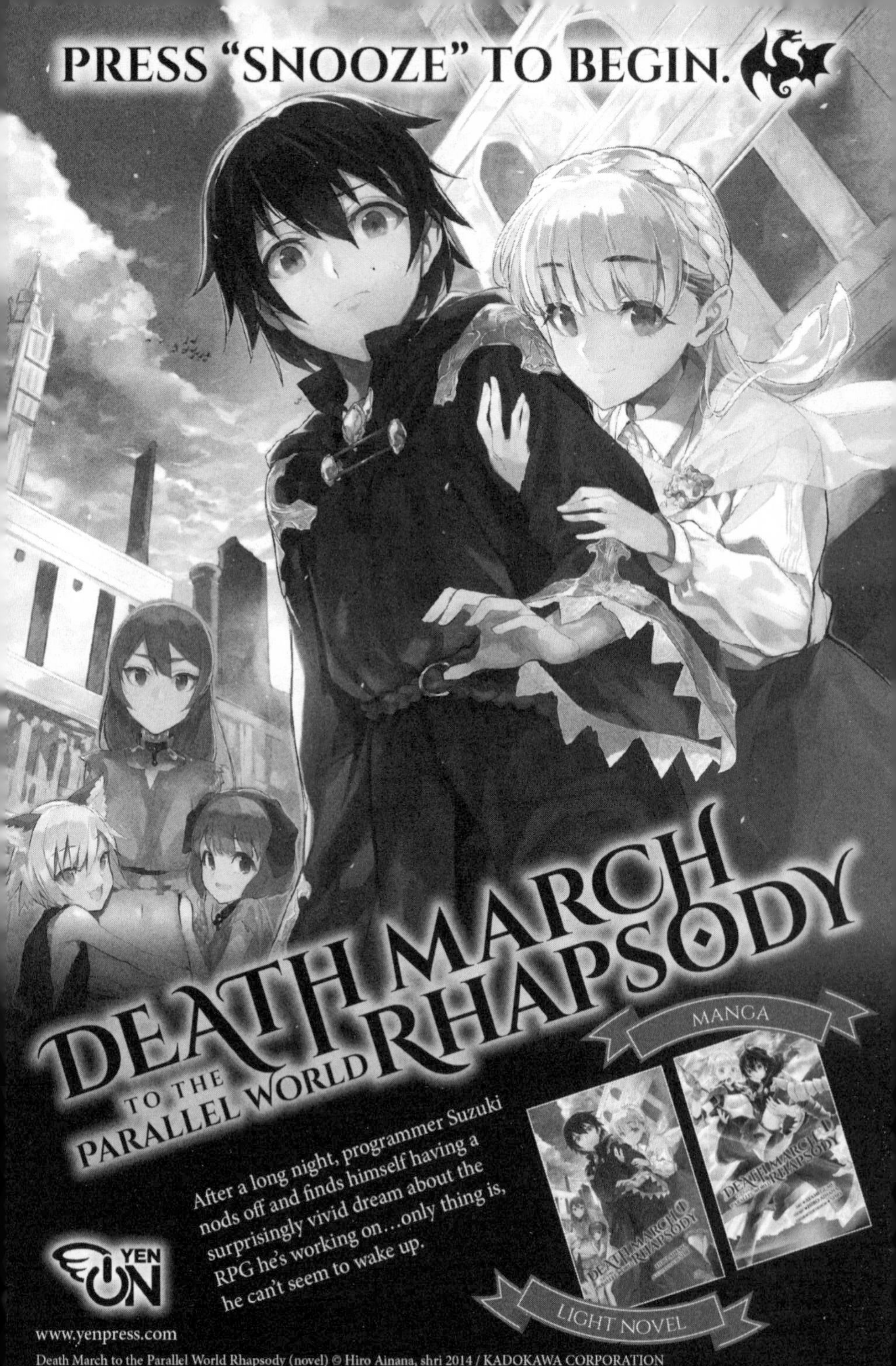
PRESS "SNOOZE" TO BEGIN.
DEATH MARCH TO THE PARALLEL WORLD RHAPSODY
MANGA
LIGHT NOVEL
After a long night, programmer Suzuki nods off and finds himself having a surprisingly vivid dream about the RPG he's working on…only thing is, he can't seem to wake up.
YEN ON
www.yenpress.com
Death March to the Parallel World Rhapsody (novel) © Hiro Ainana, shri 2014 / KADOKAWA CORPORATION
Death March to the Parallel World Rhapsody (manga) © AYAMEGUMU 2015 © HIRO AINANA, shri 2015/KADOKAWA CORPORATION

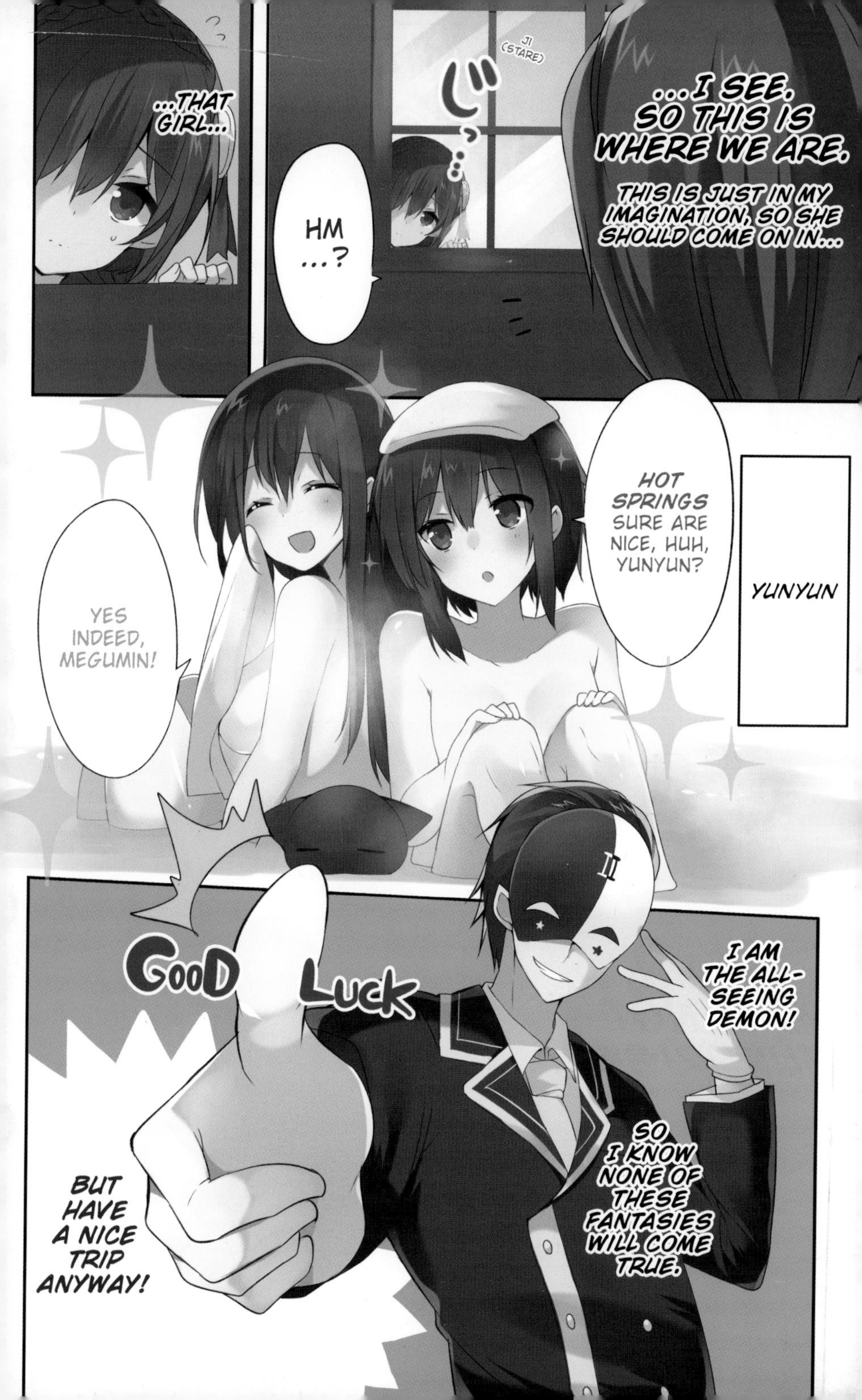
...I SEE. SO THIS IS WHERE WE ARE.
THIS IS JUST IN MY IMAGINATION, SO SHE SHOULD COME ON IN...
じっ…
JI (STARE)
HM ...?
...THAT GIRL...
YUNYUN
HOT SPRINGS SURE ARE NICE, HUH, YUNYUN?
YES INDEED, MEGUMIN!
I AM THE ALL-SEEING DEMON!
SO I KNOW NONE OF THESE FANTASIES WILL COME TRUE.
BUT HAVE A NICE TRIP ANYWAY!
GOOD LUCK

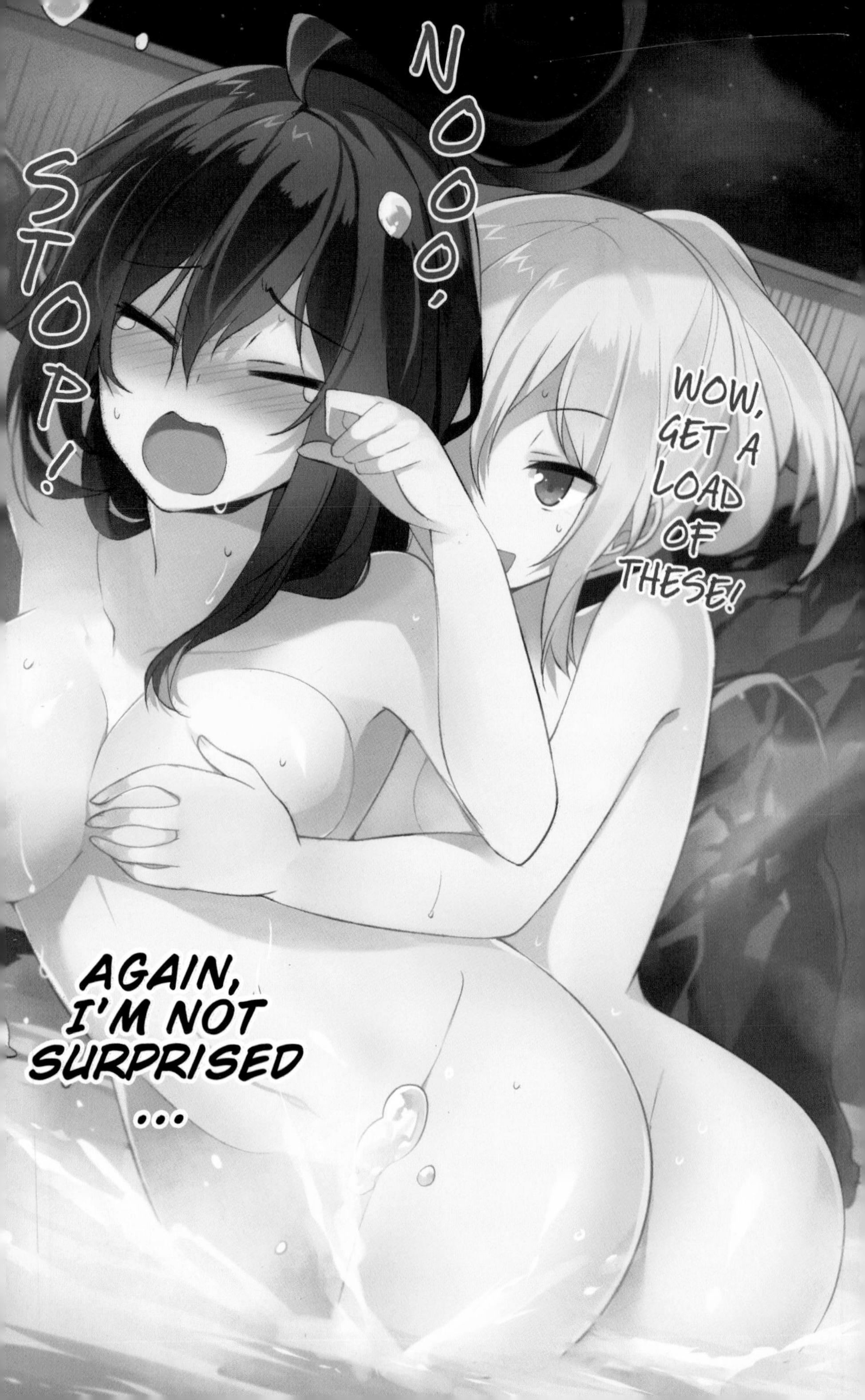
WOW, GET A LOAD OF THESE!
NOOOO,
STOP!
AGAIN, I'M NOT SURPRISED...

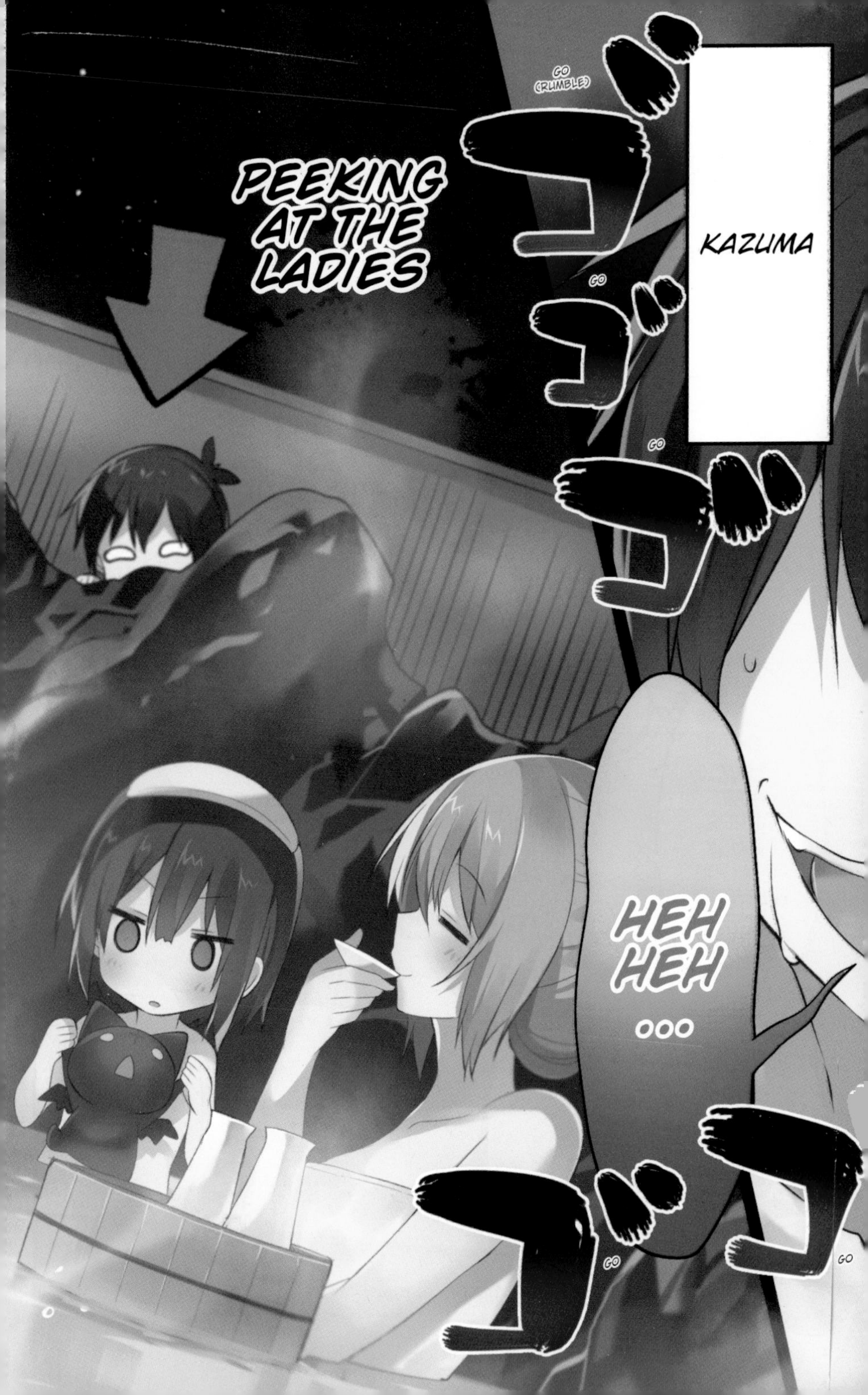

KAZUMA
GO (RUMBLE)
GO
GO
PEEKING AT THE LADIES
HEH HEH ...
GO
GO

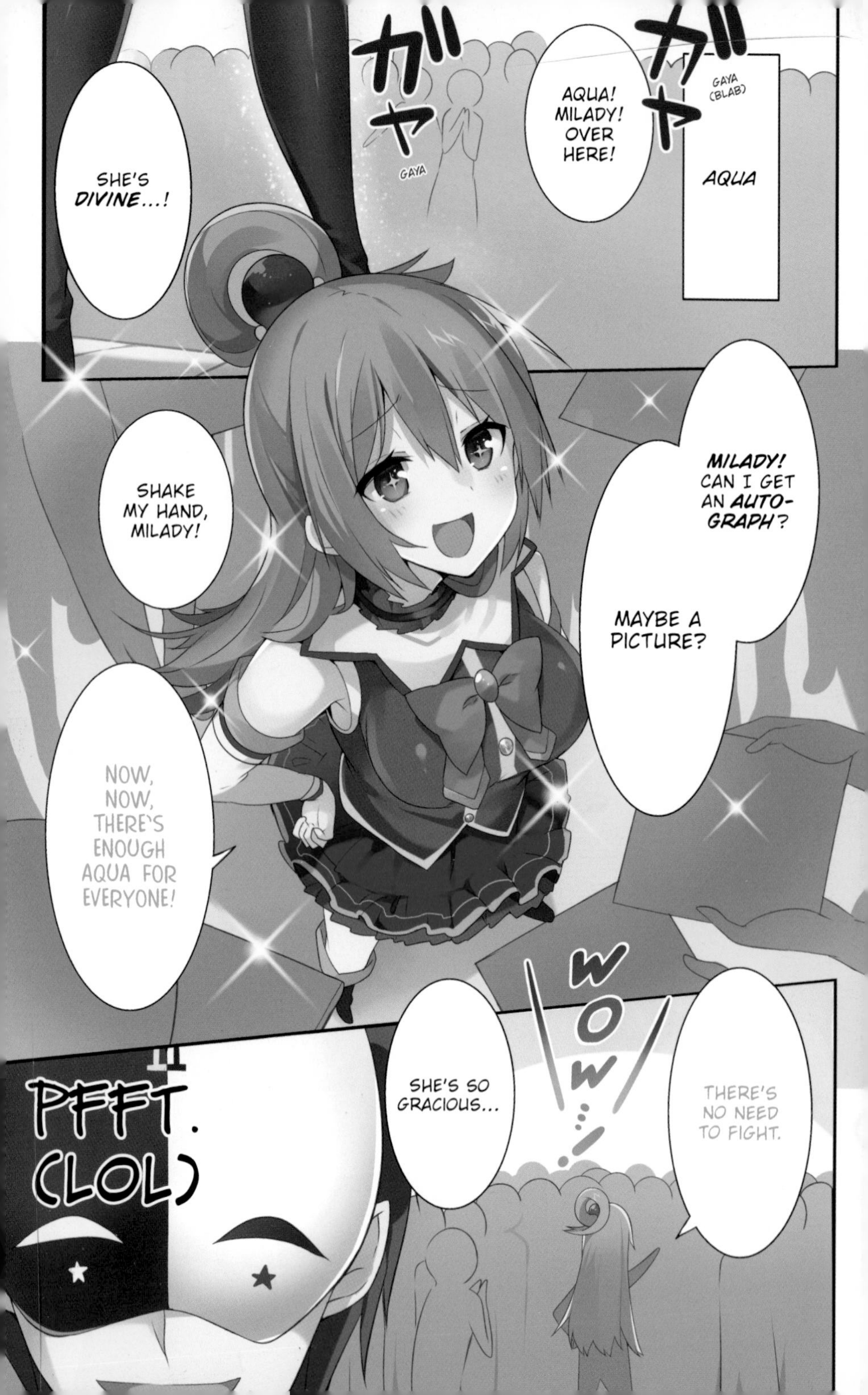
ガヤ
GAYA (BLAB)
AQUA
AQUA! MILADY! OVER HERE!
ガヤ
GAYA
SHE'S DIVINE...!
MILADY! CAN I GET AN AUTOGRAPH?
MAYBE A PICTURE?
SHAKE MY HAND, MILADY!
NOW, NOW, THERE'S ENOUGH AQUA FOR EVERYONE!
THERE'S NO NEED TO FIGHT.
WOW...!
SHE'S SO GRACIOUS...
PFFT. (LOL)

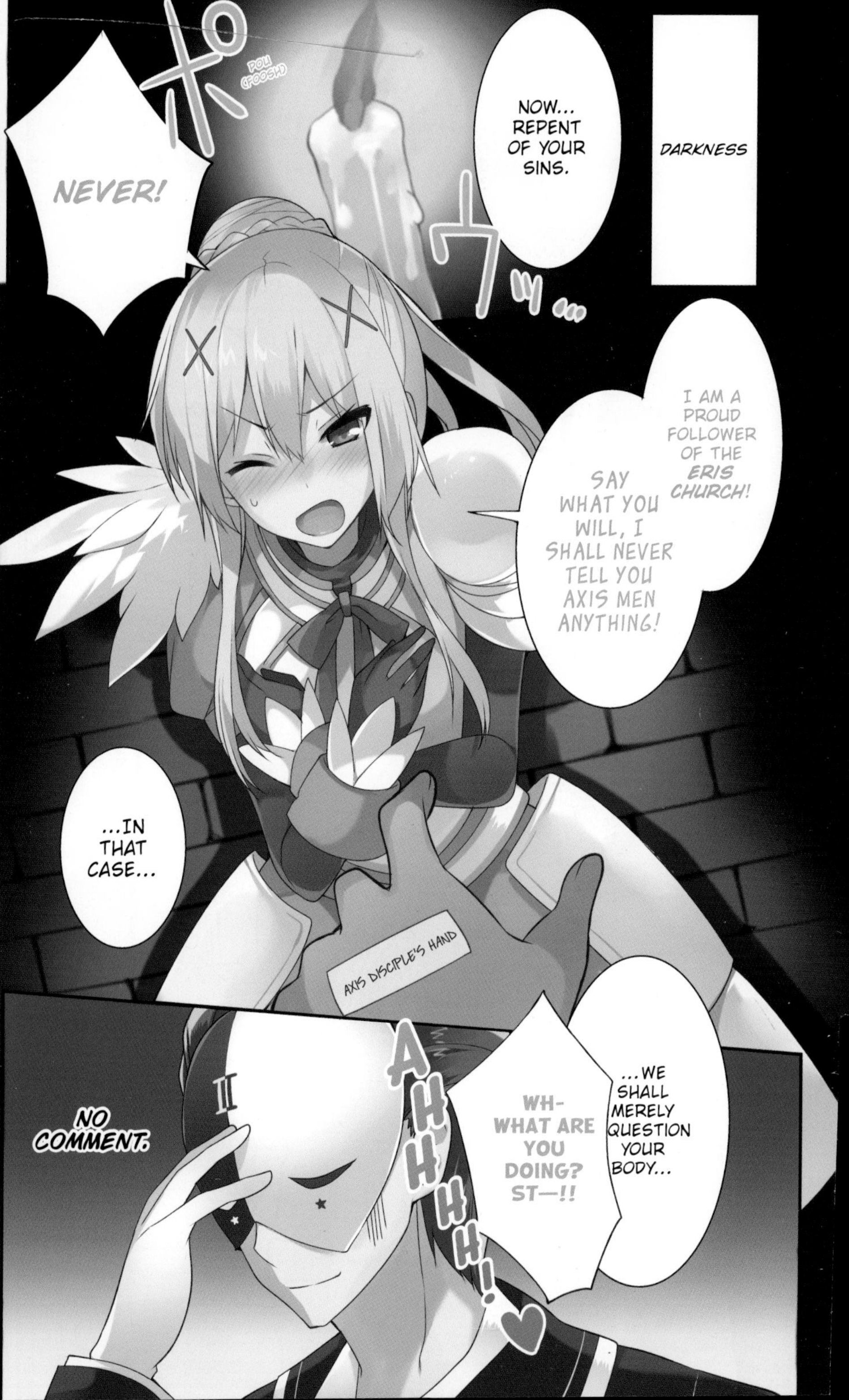
DARKNESS
NOW... REPENT OF YOUR SINS.
POU (FOOSH)
NEVER!
I AM A PROUD FOLLOWER OF THE ERIS CHURCH!
SAY WHAT YOU WILL, I SHALL NEVER TELL YOU AXIS MEN ANYTHING!
...IN THAT CASE...
AXIS DISCIPLE'S HAND
...WE SHALL MERELY QUESTION YOUR BODY...
WH- WHAT ARE YOU DOING? ST—!!
AHHHHH!♥
NO COMMENT.

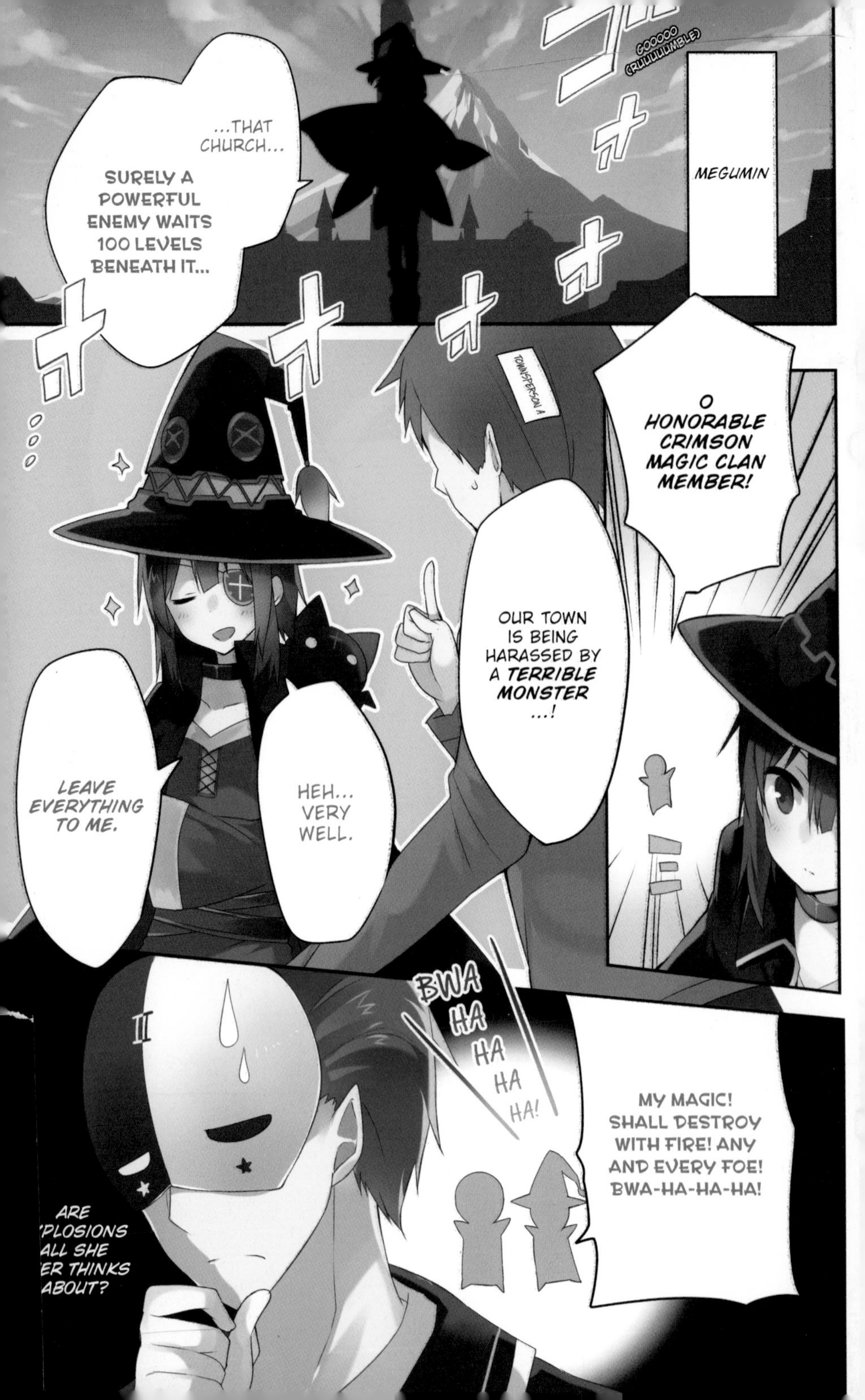
MEGUMIN
GOOOOO (RUUUUUMBLE)
...THAT CHURCH...
SURELY A POWERFUL ENEMY WAITS 100 LEVELS BENEATH IT...
TOWNSPERSON A
O HONORABLE CRIMSON MAGIC CLAN MEMBER!
OUR TOWN IS BEING HARASSED BY A TERRIBLE MONSTER ...!
HEH... VERY WELL.
LEAVE EVERYTHING TO ME.
MY MAGIC! SHALL DESTROY WITH FIRE! ANY AND EVERY FOE! BWA-HA-HA-HA!
BWA HA HA HA HA!
ARE
PLOSIONS
ALL SHE
ER THINKS
ABOUT?

TAKE THIS *LADY ERIS DOLL!* IT WILL BRING YOU *GOOD LUCK!*

YOUNG LADY, YOU LOOK *DISTRESSED*...

WIZ

♥

AND MR. VANIR DOES LOVE DOLLS, SO IT WOULD MAKE A PERFECT GIFT...

I'M SURE IT WILL MAKE THINGS MUCH EASIER AT MY SHOP...!

HMM

TRUE, I MADE DOLLS IN THE LAST VOLUME, BUT I DON'T REALLY LOVE THEM.

SHE'D PROBABLY BE MAD IF I BLEW THIS ONE UP.

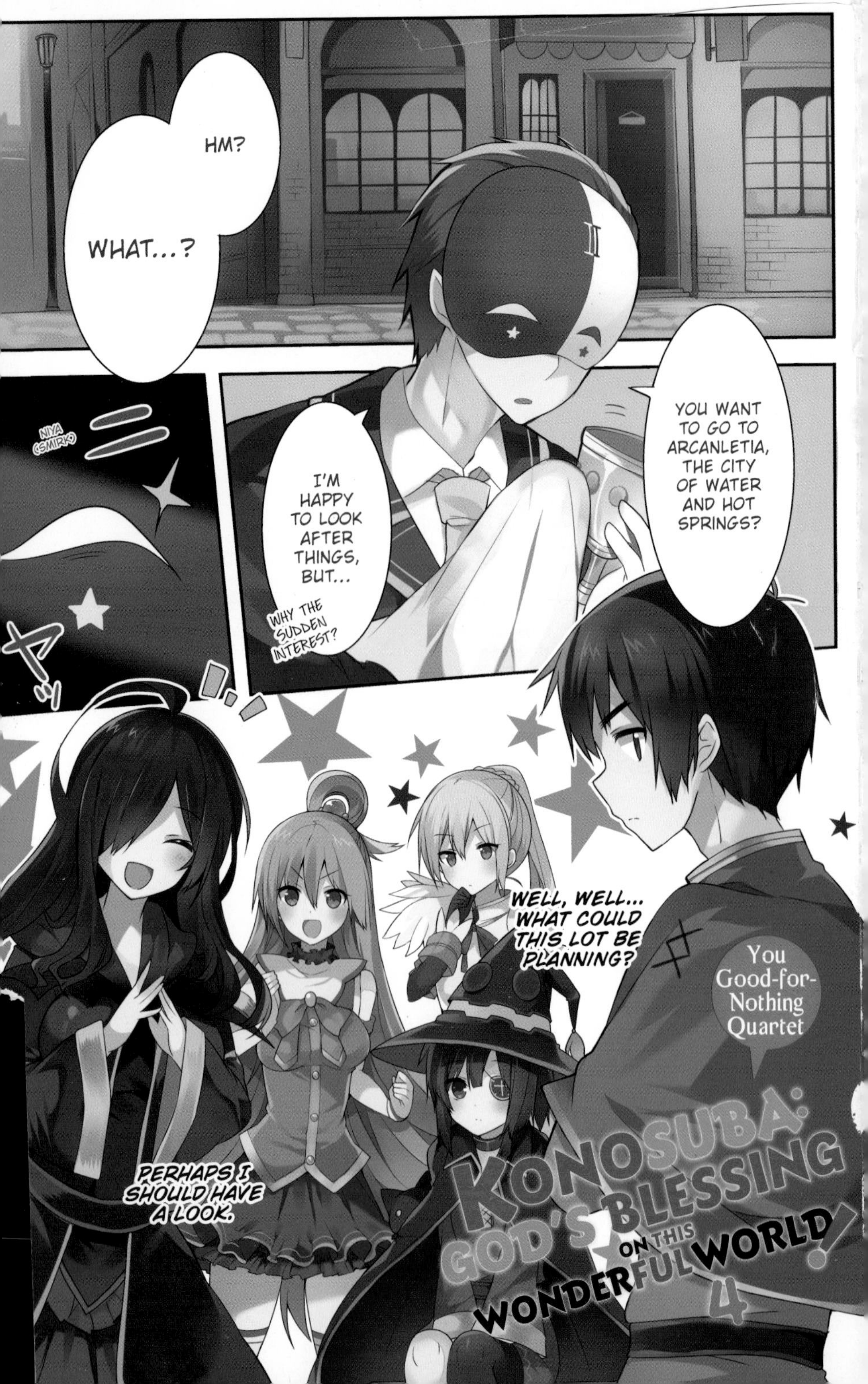
HM?
WHAT...?
YOU WANT TO GO TO ARCANLETIA, THE CITY OF WATER AND HOT SPRINGS?
I'M HAPPY TO LOOK AFTER THINGS, BUT...
WHY THE SUDDEN INTEREST?
NIYA (SMIRK)
WELL, WELL... WHAT COULD THIS LOT BE PLANNING?
You Good-for-Nothing Quartet
PERHAPS I SHOULD HAVE A LOOK.
KONOSUBA: GOD'S BLESSING ON THIS WONDERFUL WORLD! 4